Poker & Promise

PIPPA GREATHOUSE

T he wagon train, late August, 1852...

"No, no *no*..."

Betsy Lawrence held her shoulders high and her back straight as she watched shovelfuls of dirt being piled on top of the graves of her parents. Unwilling to let anyone see her tears, she waited stoically, hating the fact that they must be buried directly in the path of oncoming wagons.

Jack, the wagon master had explained that it was the safest place for them; it would keep their bodies from being devoured by wolves and other predators. Somehow that hadn't mattered; it seemed such a terrible injustice that the wagon trains from the east must roll right over them, continuing on the journey her mother and father had been so eager to make.

The cholera epidemic that had hit early in the journey had taken so many lives. It was said that if they could make it to Fort John, the Trading Post in Wyoming, the epidemic would end. The military had taken it over just that year, changing its name to Fort Laramie. When cholera struck the family in the wagon in front of them, they held out hope. But when it struck the family two wagons behind them, they began to pray. They had almost made it to Fort Laramie before Mama and Papa had become ill.

Almost.

"Elizabeth? Come away. You can't stay here, child. It's not safe."

Jerked back to reality, she turned. "I'm not a child, sir. I'm over twenty."

Jack rested his hand on her shoulder, urging her back to the wagon. He shook his head. "And I'm over twice your age. You're still a child to me. Are you sure you can drive the team?"

She wasn't sure at all, and looked around. "Is there anyone else who can do it? Without taking them away from their own?"

He didn't look at her. The drivers of the remaining

wagons were already with their teams. Those who could be spared had taken over for the families whose men were no longer living.

"I thought not," she said quietly.

Despite her determination not to show her sorrow, tears again began to threaten. She'd hoped for a few more minutes, just a few, to stand beside their graves and silently say goodbye.

But the wagons had already prepared to leave. She realized everyone was waiting on her. Clenching her jaw, she took a determined step toward the wagon. Then another. The team was restless. She'd only driven it alone a few times, and she wasn't sure she could do it for long.

There seemed, however, no other choice. The band of stragglers in the wagon train were few and far between now, and she should have known better than to ask.

You can do it, Betsy. Keep your chin up. Her mother's voice seemed to echo in her ear. *You can do anything you put your mind to. I know you.*

She climbed up onto the wagon, feeling small and alone, and took the reins from Jack.

As the train began to move forward, she kept her eyes straight ahead, closing them only as the horses trod over the graves of her parents. She wondered then how many other souls were buried here, under the hooves of the horses.

"Goodbye, Mama. Goodbye, Papa." She whispered.

No one was looking at her now, and the tears began to flow, clouding her vision. But Bess, the mare ahead of her stumbled suddenly, and Betsy jerked her head upward.

She couldn't cry. *No*. Not *now*.

She blinked, swearing to herself she wouldn't lose control of the horses. And swearing not to lose the few possessions that remained in the wagon behind her, all she had left of her family's memories.

And most of all, swearing not to look back.

few weeks later...

Fort Laramie lay before them. Betsy sighed with relief when she saw it come into view. Twice in the past two days the horses had reared on her and someone from the wagon train had been forced to ride out to get her. They were perturbed with her now, and she knew it.

The weeks since her parents' deaths had been hard. Still, she hadn't had much time to think. Driving the team was difficult, and it took every second of concentration to keep up with them. At night she'd barely had a chance to lay her head on her pillow before she fell asleep.

The fort was bustling. It looked welcoming to her. Perhaps it had a place where she could find work. Was that possible? Were there any other ladies here? She'd heard they were scarce inside the military forts.

She could sew; her mother had taught her that. The treadle was in the back of the wagon; she was so grateful she'd arrived with it intact. Perhaps she *could* stay here. Would there be a place she could find room and board?

"Hand me the reins."

Jack's voice shook her out of her thoughts, causing her to lean forward. Placing the reins in his hands, she moved out of the driver's box and began to climb down.

"Stay here, Betsy. I'll be back shortly." He secured the team to the nearby post and turned back to her.

She blinked. "Where are you going?"

He put both hands on his hips, and his jaw clenched. "It's obvious, Elizabeth. You can't continue with us. I'm sorry. I'll be back."

"Wait. Haven't I gotten better at driving the team?"

He turned back, scowling. "It's not your skill, child. It's your size. You're too small to control them." He strode away, calling out behind him. "Stay."

Betsy waited until he was a good distance away before stamping her foot.

"Stay," she echoed under her breath. "What am I, a *dog*?"

The horses were watching her curiously with their soft eyes, and she moved closer and began to stroke their velvety noses.

"Sorry if I scared you," she whispered apologetically. "I don't know what's to become of me, or of you. But I'll try my best to see you're taken care of."

What *was* to become of her? She should be able to take care of herself as long as she had a place to sleep and a place to work. But would they allow her to stay in her wagon?

Probably not.

Outside the fort she could see tents belonging to the Native Americans. It wasn't likely the captain of the garrison would allow her to sleep outside the gates, and it was just as unlikely there would be room for her *inside*.

A smile crossed her face as she thought of the poker games she'd played with her father at home. When she was ten, Mama had come into the drawing room one evening and found Betsy winning a game with Papa.

Appalled, she'd thrown up her hands. "Charles! You're not teaching that child to play poker!"

"I certainly am," Papa had replied with a wink at Betsy. "But I'm not sure I will again. She just won against me for the third time, and I'll be a pauper for the rest of my days."

Her mother had left the room, sputtering, and Betsy and Papa had been left behind, laughing. Papa had decided then to bet only horseback rides.

Her face relaxed, thinking of it.

Don't be silly. It isn't likely playing poker will be an opportunity here.

At the same time another thought occurred to her. There *was* a Trading Post here. Since she could sew, perhaps she could make her own living and sell her goods there. She hoped to meet the owner if she was allowed to stay.

Attempting to smooth back her hair, Betsy looked down, and grimaced. It had been two weeks since she'd been able to have a bath, and because of the lack of privacy on the wagon train, it had only been what her grandmother had referred to as a *birdy's bath*. What she'd give to actually soak in a tub of hot water and be able to wash her hair with real soap. She felt grimy. The braid she'd begun the day with had come loose from its ribbon and her dark blue pelisse needed washing, badly.

Betsy watched as the men in the train began to dismount and rein their teams to the posts, leaving their wives and families to begin working on dinner. She knew there was tinned food in the wagon, however, she had no appetite at all. She counted as she looked back at the wagons behind them. Not many were left. However, not far from them another train was pulling into view; *they* seemed to be in better shape. Wondering if all the wagon trains had encountered the same difficulties theirs had, she continued to wait.

Footfalls behind her brought her back to the present.

"She's a fine filly." It was Jack's voice.

Startled, she looked over her shoulder. Jack approached with another gentlemen, and her gaze lit on him. He was taller and quite handsome, with dark hair and eyes a dark sapphire blue, and his hat was held loosely in one hand.

One could get lost in those eyes, she thought.

Handsome or not, however, it didn't matter.

"You're not selling my mare, or *any* of my horses without my consent," she snapped.

The stranger transferred his hat to his other hand,

and his mouth lifted on one side.

"Spirited too, I gather."

He's not talking about my mare. He's talking about me.

Betsy narrowed her eyes at him. "Who are you?"

"Behave yourself, Elizabeth," Jack said, his voice filled with warning. "I'll introduce you. This is Thad Bridges. Thad, Elizabeth Lawrence."

Betsy took a step back.

The man referred to as Thad took a step forward.

"I..." Betsy found herself at a loss for words, "don't understand."

Jack turned to the stranger. "Shall I explain? Or will you?"

Thad motioned to him. "Be my guest."

Jack was rubbing the back of his neck uncomfortably now. He wasn't looking at her, either, a bad sign.

"It's like this, child. You're alone."

She ignored the reference to her age. "Yes sir. I'm quite aware of that," she said, with irritation in her voice.

"You need someone to take care of you."

She lifted her chin defiantly. "No sir. *I* don't believe I do."

"Think what you may. *I* believe you do, and I'm responsible for you since your parents died."

This time it was she who looked away.

Oh dear God. He's going to tell me Thad's wife has died and he has a house full of children and needs someone to raise them. That's all I need.

Her mouth flattened. She'd heard stories of this happening frequently out west; forced marriages of convenience. Suddenly every nerve in her body was taut. Straightening her shoulders, she stared back at Jack and the younger man next to him.

"All I need is a place to sleep. I have my treadle, and I can make my own living," she glanced from one to the other. "I can pay for my own meals."

Jack's gaze settled on her sternly. Thad's however, showed a crinkle at the corners of his eyes and his mouth.

"*Extremely* spirited," said Thad.

This was a nightmare, and suddenly Betsy realized she couldn't handle it anymore; she whirled away and began to run, although she had no idea where she was going. "I'm not listening to this any longer," she barked.

She heard footsteps behind her, she was sure Jack was coming after her. Her gait picked up, and she began to run faster, zig-zagging between people, horses and soldiers. The river rounded the fort on one side not far away, and she tried to avoid it.

The steps behind her increased their pace. Suddenly she felt hands around her waist and her feet lost contact with the ground. She was tossed over a hard shoulder like a sack of potatoes.

"Stop it, Jack! I'm almost twenty-two, and I can take care of myself!"

"Be still, young lady," said a threatening voice. "I've about had it with this stubborn streak of yours."

As she looked over her shoulder however, she realized the voice did not belong to Jack.

She gasped. "Put me down. *Now.*"

"I'll put you down when I'm ready. I'll say one thing for you, you little urchin. You're fast."

How dare he! She didn't even know him. But as the thought occurred to her, she felt a sharp stinging swat on her bottom. He spoke again.

"Do you want more? Because at this moment I'm inclined to give it to you."

She grunted at his question. "No."

Her hands against his back, she pushed herself up and peered behind her. It was several minutes later when she saw the front gate of the fort come into view. A few seconds after that, the wagon train was in sight.

"All right," he said, with a voice of steel. "I'm going to set you on your feet now. Don't you *dare* run off again. Hear?"

"No. I don't *hear*." She tossed back.

Another swat landed, this one harder than the last, and she was on her feet suddenly, facing Jack in the exact same spot she'd left. He looked exasperated with her. Thad was holding her in front of him, one arm around her shoulders and the other around her waist.

Jack jammed his hands into the pockets of his trousers. "You're making me tired, Elizabeth, and you're wasting my time. Are you ready to listen now?"

She looked away. "To what?"

Jack nodded toward Thad, behind her.

She was turned by her shoulders until she faced the stranger. Scowling upward, she realized how far she had to crane her neck to see his face. A sigh escaped. She supposed it was time to hear about the children she would be responsible for. "Get on with it, then. How many do you have?"

He stared down at her for a long time before speaking.

"Pardon?" His voice was low and firm.

She turned her head, but one large hand gripped her chin and turned it back to his.

She gulped. "How many children do you expect me to raise for you?"

He appeared genuinely surprised. "I have no children."

Nervously, she licked her lips. "Truly?"

"None. But I'll explain, if you'll be still and listen."

Curiosity was getting the better of her. Finally, she met his gaze. "I'm listening, then."

"All right. Here it is. I'm about to turn thirty, and I need a wife. You are alone in the world, and you need a husband to take care of you," he paused as his eyes flickered over her, "in more ways than one."

"What's that supposed to mean?" she threw back.

"It means you need someone to teach you to behave."

She ignored that. With a shake of her head, she added, "Then tell me. Why do you need a wife?"

"That's a fair question, and it deserves an answer. I'll be honest with you. If I don't marry within the next month, I'm in danger of losing my inheritance. The arrangement would benefit both of us."

"It might benefit *you*," she said, "but I doubt it would do the same for *me*." She stared at him. There were no children? Perhaps this wasn't as bad as she thought.

She tried to move away from his grip but he held on tighter.

"This is dangerous territory, Elizabeth, in case you haven't noticed. No, I have *no* children. Why do you ask? Do you not like children?"

"I like them well enough. I'm just not ready for them yet."

"I see. Well, here's what I do have. A house. Two, actually. One outside the fort, one inside. You'll be staying inside, at least until things calm down enough and I can teach you how to stay safe. There is a widow named Evaline who comes a few days a week and cooks and cleans. You won't need to do any of that. What you *will* need to do is marry me."

"Why would you want me? I have no dowry. I have *nothing*." She searched his face curiously. "All I own is in the wagon."

She half expected him to climb up into it and look it over, but he didn't. He continued studying her intently.

"You'll keep that."

He turned her and put his arm around her shoulders, walking her away from Jack. "Your wagon master offered me your team. I suppose I could always use them. I can promise you they would never be mistreated, but they'll remain your property." He paused, and stopped, turning her to face him. "There are some things I'll expect from you."

Her shoulders stiffened under his hands. "What things?"

He stopped walking. "The first. I'll expect you to

mind your manners and behave yourself."

She eyed him suspiciously. "And?"

"And I'll expect you to accommodate guests when needed. I know it's an odd request, but occasionally we have people visit, and the captain's quarters aren't quite large enough for it. Susannah Harrison can help you learn to do that."

"Who is Susannah?"

"The captain's wife. I expect you'll get along with her well. She was about as stubborn as you are now when she first arrived."

She ignored him. "And what *else* do you want from me?"

"What any man would. I'll expect you to share my bed."

Betsy became silent for a moment.

"I see. But I..."

A half smile appeared on his face. "I'll teach you. You need not worry."

Betsy felt it as her face grew hot. She knew she must be a bright shade of scarlet.

"Would you like to hear what else I expect of you?"

She couldn't meet his gaze now. "Yes."

"I expect you to do the things you like. To enjoy yourself. Do you like to read?"

Her eyes suddenly lit on his face. "I sew. I make

things. Clothes, mostly. I draw. And yes, I do read, but it isn't my favorite thing to do."

She paused. Should she tell him she was good at poker? Probably not. "I like to write poetry at times. And my father taught me to carve on wood."

He looked impressed. "As long as you let me sharpen your tools for you."

She sent an irritated glance upward. "I *know* how to sharpen my tools. I've been doing it since I was eight."

But he shook his head. "I won't have you injuring yourself, Elizabeth."

"My name," she said forcefully, "is *Betsy*. That's what I answer to. If you insist on calling me Elizabeth, don't be surprised if I ignore you."

He smiled. "I'll call you Betsy only when you behave yourself. If I call you Elizabeth, it should be a signal to you that you should mend your ways quickly or you'll be in trouble."

She tried to ease away from him, but he refused to let her go.

"What kind of trouble?" she whispered.

"Of my hand connecting with your bottom. At least until I think you've learned your lesson. Does that satisfy you as an answer?"

Betsy lowered her eyes to his chest and blinked.

"I... suppose so," she answered in a whisper. "But I won't like it."

A soft chuckle came from him. "I'd be surprised if you did." He released her chin and again moved both hands to her shoulders. "I expect it won't happen often, but I will demand that you be respectful to me. Is it possible for you to do that?"

She kept her gaze lowered. "Can I think about this?"

He drew a breath. "Unfortunately, no. Jack needs to head out early in the morning. It's imperative you make up your mind *now*. If you agree, we'll be married this afternoon."

"He's already told me I can't go with them when they leave," she grumbled.

"Yes. He told me that too. I'm a fair man, Betsy, as you'll find out. However, I expect you need to see that for yourself. But I can make you some promises."

She was stalling for time. "What promises?"

"I promise to take good care of you. I'll treat you well. I'll do my best to see you're happy. I'll never lie to you, and I'll expect you to do the same for me. And if you encounter a problem, I'll expect you to come to me with it. I'll take care of it for you. We'll sit down often and talk about your needs, and how I can meet them."

She tilted her head. "Why must you marry before your thirtieth birthday?"

His mouth flattened. "My father dictated it in his will. If I don't, the entire estate goes to my younger brother. He would either sell it out from under me, or bring it to ruin in a short time. I've overlooked the estate since I turned twenty, and made it prosper. My brother tried for years to talk my father into rewriting the will, He was unsuccessful, and my father died two years ago. Right now, it's in the hands of a solicitor in New York."

"Where does your brother live?"

"On the east coast. He's never been here, and he assumes we're an uncivilized lot." His mouth lifted in that same half-smile, and despite herself, she found she thought it was charming. "I've never been able to convince him to visit. It wouldn't surprise me, however, if he didn't show up around my birthday to claim the estate he thinks should fall to him. He's quite sure I'll never marry."

Betsy looked up as he chuckled. She could not deny he was a handsome man.

"I have two questions, then," she said. "Why is he so sure? And," she breathed, "why *haven't* you married?"

"You're a curious girl, aren't you?"

"Yes. It's the best way to find out what I want to know."

The amused expression was replaced with a frown. "Fair enough. The truth? I've never found a young woman I wanted."

"Are you..." her voice dropped, "sure you want *me*?"

He grinned. "No. But I think you're honest, I like your spirit, and we seem to be stuck with each other. I'm not a wealthy man by any means, but I am comfortable. I hope you understand the difference. And I hope you know I'll take good care of you. If there's something you want, tell me and I'll do the best I can to make it happen."

Betsy's mouth twisted into a sly smile. "I want to see the ocean, and hear the waves crash up on the beach." She watched for his reaction as he considered it. Silence followed as he observed her face.

"Is that truly what you want? Somehow, I have doubts about that."

"Yes." She was lying, and he knew it. She could tell by the look on his face. "No," she finally added, looking down. "What I truly want is my parents back. But *you* can't give me that."

Her lower lip trembled as he stood there gazing

down at her. His hands continued to rest on her shoulders, but his grip had lessened.

"No, I can't. I'm sorry. If I could, I would." There was silence for a few seconds. "And it's not what I expected to hear. Taking you to see the west coast would be easier. There are rumors of two men in the east, Wells and Fargo, who plan to send the stage west since the railroad doesn't come here yet. Perhaps eventually they'll do that. I can't make that promise to you yet, Betsy. But if it becomes possible, I'll do the best I can."

This was something she hadn't expected. "You're serious?"

"I am. The question is now," he said, "will you accept my offer of marriage?"

She studied his face curiously. He appeared sincere. There wasn't a houseful of children to have to step in and raise and try to convince they should let her take the place of their mother. She didn't even have to be responsible for the housekeeping. Surely, she could get Susannah to teach her to entertain. She could do whatever she wanted as long as she, as he put it, *behaved herself*.

"It depends," she said, a moment later. "I'm curious. What do you mean when you say 'If I behave myself?'"

"I'll tell you. It means coming to me when I call you. It means keeping a respectful attitude in front of others *and* when we're alone. You can voice a disrespectful opinion in private, but in the presence of others, mind your tongue. It means being pleasant to be around. I don't expect you to address me as sir, but respect needs to be present in your manner. As I said before, I'll need you to entertain guests occasionally. I'll give you plenty of notice, and Evaline can help prepare the dishes to serve, but you'll need to learn how to plan it and serve it." He glanced down at her soiled gown and pelisse. "If you need new gowns made, I'll be happy to provide them."

"I have some in the wagon, but they're for every day. If it's necessary to have new garments to entertain in, I can make them. But I might need the goods."

"I'll see you get them. And when we have guests, I'll expect you to stay close by my side. It's all about respect, Betsy."

"That's all?"

There was a pause before he answered. "No. That's not all. I've had a few years to think about what I want from a marriage. I promise I'll always try to put you first, and I expect the same from you. I apologize for having to rush you into this. Any other questions?"

She lowered her head. "Can I have a bath any time

I want one? It's just—on the wagon train..." She looked up at his chuckle. "And do you have a place I can use to sew?"

"The bath? Any time you wish, I promise. The room to sew? There's a room at the top of the stairs that might fit your needs. If not, you can use one of the bedrooms. You're an easy one to please."

"No, I'm *not* really. But thank you." Betsy tried to make her voice sound satisfied. Inside, however, her mind was whirling. What if he was not all he presented to be? What if he was too demanding, too harsh, too...

She gave him another glance. He *looked* sincere. But what if he wasn't?

The answer was clear. Then, she'd leave, she promised herself. She'd run away. Surely wagon trains came and went all the time from Fort Laramie. She'd save her money and stow away on one as it left.

Yes. She could do this.

She nodded, suddenly, surprising even herself.

"Then I accept."

"Good girl."

Betsy was surprised at the feeling of pleasure his words evoked. The urge to smile up at him was strong. But she didn't. She kept her head lowered, wondering what the rest of the day would bring.

Chapter Two

A few moments later...

Betsy allowed Thad to take her by the hand and lead her across the compound toward a log house. It wasn't large, however, it did have an upper floor. She studied it as they approached. It was stark. The curtains at the downstairs windows were rather drab. She supposed men weren't picky about the materials used in things like curtains. There seemed to be none at all visible in the windows upstairs.

"This is my home away from home," he explained, as he opened the front door and led her inside. "As you can see, it needs a woman's touch. Since you sew, perhaps you can add it." Raising his voice, he looked toward the back of the house. "Evie?"

A woman who looked to be in her forties appeared with a towel in her hands. "Cooking your lunch, Thad."

"Good. I hope there's enough for the three of us." He led Betsy into the kitchen. "Evaline Jones, meet Elizabeth Lawrence. We'll be getting married this afternoon."

Betsy stared at him as he made the announcement. If it was a surprise to Evaline, she didn't show it. The woman smiled at her. "I made plenty for lunch. And the name is *Evie*."

Betsy smiled back. "And mine is Betsy, even though Thad doesn't seem to want to use it."

Evie's friendly grin answered. "I guess you'll be wanting a bath before the ceremony? There's a tub in the back room."

A *bath*? Betsy immediately smiled back. "Oh, yes, ma'am. I'd like that *very* much."

"Well, let's get you fed then. When you've eaten, we'll pour the bath."

Thad gave her a nod. "If you'll heat the water, I'll carry it to the tub."

Evie paused, bringing another set of dishes to the table. "Do you have a frock that's suitable?"

Betsy remembered her mother's wedding dress, packed away somewhere amidst the crates. Of all the things in the wagon, it was probably the only appropriate frock she owned, however, her mother had been tall; she doubted it would fit her without several alterations. "I don't know," she said, creases furrowing her brow.

A knock on the door startled her.

"It's all right. It'll be Jack with your things." Thad strode across the room to open it. Jack was the first to enter, followed by several other men. Each of them carried a crate of things from the wagon. Even though she'd helped pack them, she wasn't certain exactly what each crate held.

"Where do you want these?" Jack asked.

But Thad shook his head. "I'll show you," he said, leading them through the kitchen and to the right. Opening a doorway, he motioned toward the inside. "Through here. Just set them down next to the wall. After Betsy's had a chance to look through them, she can decide where they should go. But there's no need to do that right now."

Betsy could have wept with relief at Thad's words. He winked at her as Evie showed the men where to put things. "You might want to go upstairs and take a look at the rooms there. You can decide where you'd like to set up your sewing."

As she nodded, he left her to explore the house and followed the men back to the wagon.

Quietly Betsy ascended the stairs. It might be better to get out of everyone's way while they brought her things in.

The staircase was steep and narrow, but there was at least a banister secured to it. The top opened up into a small cozy room with one window; perhaps this was one she could use for sewing. Off that, there was a larger room with a small bed and a closet. Betsy peeked inside and turned back to the one at the top of the stairs. There was room for a cutting table and a board to press things. There wasn't much in it right now. A rocker sat next to the window, and she moved to stand by it, looking out.

From there, she could see this side of the fort. Jack and Thad were approaching, carrying the hope chest that had belonged to her mother. Other men were following, their arms full of crates. Jack was smiling; something she hadn't seen him do much of over the past few months. She hoped things looked better for him from here westward.

She stood there long enough to watch them bring in the treadle, followed by a small stack of quilts. Other things passed by, some she recognized as belonging to her mother; some her father. Tears tugged at the backs of her eyes.

Stop it, Betsy. You're becoming maudlin.

Moving away, she went into the other room.

Like the downstairs, it too could use a woman's touch. She wondered if there were enough goods left to make new curtains for them. When she heard the men below, she went back into the small upstairs room and lowered herself into the rocker, staring out the window.

A voice spoke above her suddenly; a soft gracious voice she'd never heard before.

"You look lost."

Brought back to the present, she jumped. She hadn't even heard footfalls on the stairs.

"Pardon?"

A young woman stood near the top of the staircase, smiling.

"I'm Susannah. Call me Suzy. Thad said I might find you up here." The words were spoken so kindly, Betsy gulped. It was hard to keep her eyes from filling with tears.

"I'm Betsy."

"I know. Thad told me. He's a good friend of my

husband's. Welcome, Betsy. It's good to have you here. I hope we can be friends."

"He told me about you, too. He said you could teach me how to..." She found herself searching for the words Thad had used. "*Accommodate* guests."

Suzy smiled. "That, I can do. What else did he tell you?"

Betsy hesitated. "That you were wild when you came here. As much as I am now." She frowned, suddenly. "No, wait. That's not what he said. *Stubborn* was the word he used."

"He didn't!" Susannah shook her head, grinning. "I'll put senna in his tea the next time he visits."

"You will *not*." Thad's deep voice spoke from farther down the stairs, and they looked down to see him carrying up a stool. "Be nice, or I'll tell Andrew."

Suzy laughed and shook her head as she wandered into the small room. "It's lovely up here. I've always liked this room." She glanced back toward Betsy, patting her hand. "Call me Suzy. We'll talk. And yes, I'll teach you to entertain company if you'll teach me to sew. I saw the treadle being carried inside." The tone in her voice was mischievous. "But we can do that later. Would you like me to help you get ready for the ceremony this afternoon? A wedding should be a special occasion, and I *may* have a gown you could wear for it if you don't already have one."

"I have my mother's," Betsy returned, "somewhere. But I doubt it would fit me."

Suzy turned to glance at Thad. "What time is the wedding?"

He shook his head. "Father Timothy said around two. Can you and the captain stand up with us? And Betsy, can you be ready?"

Suddenly feeling embarrassed, she looked away. "As long as there's time for a bath."

Susannah patted her shoulder. "I'm sure Andrew will be happy to stand up as a witness. And Betsy, I'll be back by one, with a gown you can use in case you don't find yours."

"Thank you, Suzy." Betsy sighed with relief.

Thad glanced from Suzy to her. "You two will get along well. Come, Betsy,' he said, reaching for her hand, "Evaline has dinner ready. Did you eat breakfast this morning?"

Betsy only nodded. She wasn't about to tell him she hadn't eaten since yesterday.

Thad eyed her curiously during the meal. She seemed determined to remain quiet, although she did make one or two polite comments about how wonderful the food was. And if she had indeed eaten breakfast, she couldn't have eaten much. She was rapidly downing the food as if she hadn't eaten in days, not hours. He couldn't help but smile at her behavior. To have been so vocal when he'd thrown her over his shoulder and smacked her bottom this morning, she was extremely quiet now.

He forced back a smile as he studied her. Under all that grime was a young woman he suspected was beautiful. The sun was now moving toward the west, and brought out strands of fire in her hair he wanted to touch. It would be interesting to see her after her bath.

When she finally set her fork down and asked if she could help with the dishes, he shook his head.

"I'm sure Evaline would appreciate the help, but time is short. If you want a bath, it's now or never.."

Betsy looked up. "I'll hurry. Can I help fill the tub?"

"*I'll* fill it. The big pots are too heavy for you." Thad rose from his chair and disappeared through a doorway to the back, carrying one of the pots he had picked up from the stove. By the time he'd added the hot water to the cool, Betsy was dancing on her feet.

"How long has it been since you bathed in a tub?" he asked.

Embarrassed, Betsy shook her head.

"Too long," was all she said.

The bath should have been a relaxing experience; instead, it was anything *but*. Betsy had seen the load of things the men had put into the back room; there was barely room for the tub now. Her heart sank as she realized she'd never be able to lay her hands on a clean frock for her wedding. It would be a miracle if she could even find a clean chemise to wear.

She prayed Suzy would be able to bring something over with her when she came.

The thought had barely occurred to her when she finished washing her hair in the chamomile soap, and rinsing it with the rose-scented tea Evie had managed to borrow for her.

Ah, but she felt clean! *Clean*, for the first time she could remember since she'd left home.

No one had told her how grimy a girl could get on a wagon train, cooking over a campfire and not being able to bathe properly.

She stiffened, hearing a voice outside, and then

realized it was Suzy. Seconds later there was a knock on the door.

"Betsy?" Suzy's head appeared around the door. "It's me. I brought you some things."

"Oh, Suzy, thank you. All of my clothes are hidden away."

"I know. I saw the men bringing in all the crates, and I knew you might never be able to locate a suitable gown. Anyway, this one was given to me to wear. It came from Joseph the Longhunter. I hope you don't mind. He got it in trade from Old Mrs. Worthington who didn't have any use for it, so he gave it to me. It's really lovely. You'll meet Joseph soon. He's our local trapper and trader."

Betsy looked at the gown with longing. It was decorated beautifully with lace and satin, even though it appeared a little long. "I can never thank you enough," she whispered.

Suzy grinned. "I can tell what you're thinking. Yes, it's a bit long for you, and there isn't much time to alter it, but we'll do the best we can. Oh, and I brought you a garter, too. It was also one I didn't use. And look, I brought a set of jeweled hair combs. You can have these. I never wear them. Thad will want you to wear your hair down, if I know him."

Thad. Betsy felt guilty, suddenly. He was as much a

victim in this situation as she. The very least she could do was to try to please him.

Evie handed in two large towels, and Suzy took them and began drying Betsy's hair.

"You have such lovely hair," she said softly.

Betsy smiled. "Thank you. Wagon trains must be the grimiest way in the world to travel."

"Agreed. Where did you come from?" Suzy asked.

"Virginia. You?"

"Boston."

Betsy gave a mock bow. "You *win*."

Suzy laughed. "I *should*. It was a horrible trip. I left way more dirt and (grime) on the tub when I arrived than you. The only redeeming thing about being on a wagon train was the scenery. Oh, I brought you these, too." She turned away and began opening the pile of things she'd brought in as Betsy climbed out of the tub. "I found you a clean chemise, too. You can keep it until you locate yours."

Betsy glanced at the lovely things Suzy had brought with her. "Oh, Suzy. You're a godsend."

Suzy, however, shook her head. "No. Just someone who's been there before and knows what you might need."

Betsy finished drying and reached for garments Suzy held out. "Tell me about Thad. Please."

Suzy's thoughtful glance met hers.

"I'll tell you what I know. He's a good man, and you're a lucky woman." She leaned forward, whispering. "And if I hadn't already fallen for Andrew, I might have had thoughts about him. The truth is, though, he's strict."

"And your husband isn't?"

"He pretends to be." A giggle escaped Suzy. "But I've learned how to get around him pretty well. Thad, now; he's a different story. I think you'll have a bit of trouble talking your way out of trouble with him. Here, if you'll stand, I'll brush out your hair and finish hemming the gown."

A knock on the door caused both to turn. Suzy hurried to it and opened it just a crack.

"She's not dressed. You can't see her."

"Pardon?" Thad's voice was deep

Betsy watched as Suzy ignored his question. "What time is it?" she asked.

"Twenty before two. You need to hurry. It'll take ten minutes to walk to the chapel.

"You needn't wait," Suzy threw back. "We'll be there on time."

"I'm waiting. I'll escort my bride to the chapel." His voice was firm, and Suzy rolled her eyes heavenward as she turned to Betsy.

"See what I mean?" she mouthed before turning back to the door. "You'd better send Evie in to help, then."

There was a pause, and the door closed. A few seconds later it opened, and Evie entered. "Thad says to hurry!" She whispered.

Thad was pacing up and down in the kitchen outside the door when it opened, and she stepped out.

He halted mid-step and stared at his bride.

She was *beautiful*. Her skin was flushed a delicate pink, and the gown she wore accented her tiny waist. Her blonde hair seemed to be a combination of several colors, and the fiery red strands he'd noticed earlier were still there, looking as if the sun had swept down and kissed them. Two delicate jeweled combs adorned the sides of her hair, bringing back the soft curls from the sides. In the back, it fell softly down, ending near her waist, and he had difficulty refraining from touching it.

There were faint little freckles that marched across the bridge of her nose. One thing was clear however.

She was absolutely adorable.

He noticed something else, too. She was trembling. Reaching her, he put an arm around her to steady her.

"Are you ready?"

"No." As if realizing what she'd said, she gave a slight shake of her head.

He chuckled. "It's all right. I did ask." Looking behind her at Suzy and Evaline, he smiled. "Ladies? Time to go."

Evie, however, shook her head. "I'll stay behind and make a dessert for your guests."

"That will be nice. Thank you. But it's happening so suddenly, I have doubts anyone else will be there."

"I think you may be astonished." Suzy's response surprised him.

"Really?"

"I'm serious. I ran into the twins on the way back home earlier. They wanted to know what was going on and weren't about to accept anything but the truth."

"Ah. I see. So now the whole of Laramie knows about the wedding." He held out his arm to Betsy with a wink. "If Permelia and Cordelia know? *Everyone* knows."

"And if you don't want to tell them something," Suzy added, "they sense it, and immediately want to know more about it. So, the best thing to do is to put a hand to your head and claim you have *the headache*.

Then they'll pat you on the shoulder and say, 'There, there'. And let you go."

Betsy laughed, and Thad looked down at her, smiling at the delightful sound. He wondered how long it had been since she'd last laughed; Weeks? *Months?*

The door to the chapel was open when they reached it, Betsy was still hanging on his arm, although she seemed to be holding on with fingers that were slightly tight. Was she nervous? That was a ridiculous thought; of *course,* she was.

He hoped she would open up and talk to him before long.

But it didn't appear that was likely to happen. Not any

time soon.

"I..." Betsy gulped and took a deep breath. "I *do.*"

It had taken her several seconds to get the words out, and she'd done it only because she didn't want to embarrass Thad in front of his friends. The church, after all, was full. Apparently, Permelia and Cordelia had done their job well. Warily, she glanced up to see if Thad was angry with her for taking so long.

If he was, he didn't show it. His face held... what? Tenderness? Surely another man would be upset with her for her hesitation over the vows. But when she'd finished, his smile rewarded her.

"Ladies and gentlemen, may I introduce to you to Mr. and Mrs. Thaddeus Bridges."

Thad leaned down into her ear.

"I'll take you back to the house. Sorry, but we need to meet a few people. I didn't anticipate the chapel being so full."

She let a small giggle escape. "Permelia and Cordelia?"

He grinned. "Exactly. Come, Mrs. Bridges."

It was easy to spot the twin sisters. They appeared to be in their forties, and approached with a bounce in their steps. They dressed alike and looked identical, and both missed the same tooth on one side. Betsy couldn't help staring as they came forward.

"Oh, greetings, my dears," said one. "I'm Cordelia. I'm the eldest."

"And I'm Permelia," said the other. "I'm the youngest." They both looked at each other and let out a giggle. "Did you enjoy the chapel being full?"

"Indeed," said Thad. "Thank you."

"And you, my dear," Cordelia nodded toward

Betsy. "Where did you come from? Thad never told us he had a sweetheart."

Betsy wondered if perhaps she should claim to have *the headache*, but decided against it.

"I came from Philadelphia," she lied, ignoring the way Thad glanced down at her.

"Oh! Oh! Such a wonderful town. It's where we're from. Isn't it, Permelia?"

"Oh yes! I don't suppose you've ever met the Blankenships?" At the shake of Betsy's head, she continued, "They were shipbuilders from England. No? Or the Raines? Or the..."

She continued on, as Betsy continued to shake her head. Finally, Thad smiled.

"Elizabeth has been complaining of the headache this afternoon. I probably should get her home. But please feel free to come by. Evaline is making dessert for everyone."

"Oh, there, *there*," Cordelia patted Betsy's arm, "You really should lie down for a spell. Shouldn't she, Permelia?"

"Yes, indeed." Permelia's head bobbed up and down, and Thad smiled.

"I'll insist on it," he said softly. "Thank you so much for the advice. See you there."

Betsy managed to keep a straight face until she was

out of the chapel. Then she paused. It was more likely they were just eager to see who in the world Thad had decided to marry. Then she pulled him behind one of the buildings and plastered both hands over her mouth before she began laughing.

"You, my girl," he said, "are a terrible liar. If you're going to insist on doing it, I'll have to teach you to do it properly."

"I should have known better," she said in a whisper. Now, they'll be asking me about all the landmarks there I've never seen."

"That'll teach you to lie. Next time, tell the truth."

"But—" she sputtered. "That's not fair. *You* lied when you told them I had the headache."

"Trust me, young lady," he said firmly, "By the time you meet everyone who comes to the house, it'll be the truth."

Betsy scowled at him, but only briefly. At the moment, however, she could already feel pain building behind her eyes

Father O'Leary was the first to greet them as he came in with a big smile.

"Ah, Thaddeus," he said, his Irish accent noticeable. "If I'd known such a lovely lady would be in Fort Laramie, I'd have come as a soldier instead of entering the priesthood." He winked at Betsy and moved on to greet the other guests as if the house was his own.

The twins were next, coming in on the arm of a handsome gentleman. He immediately reached for Betsy's hand, kissing it.

"Ah, hello, my lady. Lieutenant Will Brent, at your service." His smile was genuine, and Betsy smiled back.

"Come in, Will." Thad drew Betsy closer to his side. A moment later, he bent down to her ear, whispering. "I think I'm going to have to lock you away from view, after all."

Evie came forward, handing each of them a cup filled with liquid. "It's lemonade," she whispered. I feared you'd become thirsty. And the cake is finished. There is a bit of food in the kitchen for the guests as well."

Betsy turned. Evie was right. She'd prepared a feast, and Susannah was guiding the guests toward the kitchen.

Betsy stared at all the people who were standing outside waiting to enter, wondering how many of these people were from the fort. Or had they come from the wagon trains passing through? She didn't know.

Thad *was* right, after all. Within an hour, her head was pounding furiously.

She forced a smile to her lips as she greeted them. But when she couldn't stand it any longer, she rose on tiptoe and whispered into Thad's ear.

"It's come true. I feel bad for leaving you, but is there a place I can lie down in quiet for a little while?"

He eyed her. "In our bedroom, sweetheart."

She looked around, confused, and he bent down to her ear.

"Come with me. I'll take you." Wrapping her fingers firmly in his, he led her toward the hallway next to the stairwell. Reaching behind it, he grasped a knob and opened it. Betsy was surprised; had she not seen him open the door, she doubted she'd have known the room was even there.

Betsy glanced around. In the corner across from them was a large feather bed adorned with a colorful quilt. To her right was a large wardrobe, and to her left, a highboy. A charming secretary stood in the corner with little pockets built into it, filled with stationery. An inkwell of green glass was on the desk, full of ink, and a quill lay next to it. Betsy decided the house was deceptive. It didn't appear quite so large from the outside. Thad closed the door behind them and led her toward the bed, guiding her down to sit on the edge.

"Told you so," he said softly. "I suspect most of these folks came from wagon trains passing through. Father Timothy loves gatherings, and he'll invite anyone who will come. I'll lock the door. I can get back in, but no one else can, so you won't be bothered. Close your eyes and take a rest, sweetheart. When they discover their bride is missing, perhaps they'll leave. Understand?"

"Yes, thank you." She nodded, whimpering at the pain the motion caused.

Closing her eyes, she barely remembered the sound of the key in the lock.

Chapter Three

T *ough versus tender...*

Thad had just locked the door to the bedroom when he remembered the curtains had been left parted. He wondered if the light might make her headache worse and quietly went back in. Striding toward the window, he pulled the drapery together to darken the room further. As he passed the bed, he noticed her eyes were already closed in sleep.

"Betsy?"

No answer.

"Elizabeth," he called softly.

There was still no answer. He stood there a moment watching her, and smiled. That adorable little mouth begged to be kissed. After all, he'd already informed her he expected her in his bed, hadn't he? He'd let her recover before he demanded her body as his, but as he moved back toward the doorway, he stopped. Her tiny waist and innocent face called to him, and he couldn't help but take the few strides back to the bed.

Lifting first one hand, then the other, he kissed each palm, then smiled again. The freckles across the bridge of her nose didn't show in the dim light, but he leaned down and kissed each cheek, then the tip of her nose. Before he left, he bent once more to kiss her forehead, letting his lips linger there a moment.

But a moment was all he could spare; noise from the guests in the rest of the house demanded his attention.

With a sigh, he again locked the door and dropped the key into his pocket. Glancing around the staircase to see what was happening, he moved toward the drawing room.

Permelia and Cordelia had taken over, and were explaining to the guests that the bride had developed *the headache*, and the groom was putting her to bed. A hush was slowly descending over the house at the news, and it had already begun emptying out.

Thad smiled. For the first time, the twins had earned his complete appreciation.

* * *

That afternoon...

Thad said goodbye as the last visitor left the house. Evaline had showed him the delightful supper meal she'd prepared for them, and took her leave, too.

Her feet seemed to drag as she moved toward the door. "I... don't suppose you'll be needing me any longer," she said, turning to face him.

"Indeed? I'd like it very much if you kept your schedule and your duties, just as you are now."

She looked surprised. "But since you've a wife now..."

He put a hand on her shoulder. "Betsy is young, Miss Evie. She's just recently lost both her parents to cholera and she's been through a grueling time. She's struggled to drive a team of horses for the last few weeks. The wagon master said she couldn't continue traveling with them. The last thing she wanted was to marry me." He paused. "It would be good of you to stay and keep her company for as long as you can. She wants to see the ocean, and she's given up her life to marry me. I expect she has no idea how to keep a house or cook, although she says she sews. I hate to throw her into being responsible for everything just yet. Susannah offered to teach her how to entertain guests, but if you'd be so kind, she'll need you to help prepare the dishes."

She brightened. "Poor dear. Certainly. I'll be glad to stay. Shall I come tomorrow?"

"Please. She'll need to be going through her things to decide what to keep and what to take to the cabin. The Sioux and the Cheyenne are restless right now, and I won't be able to be here much during the day."

She nodded. "I'll be here in the morning promptly at seven, then."

"Thank you," he added, "for everything. You saved the day with the wedding feast this afternoon. I wasn't prepared for the number of guests we had."

She gave him a big smile as she left, and he closed the door after her.

He had his little bride all to himself now. Moving to the bedroom, he took out the key and opened the door.

Betsy was lying on the bed with her face turned

toward him. The look of discomfort was gone from her countenance now; she looked peaceful and innocent as she slept. It was the first time he'd seen that expression. Slowly he lit the lamp and approached the bed, being careful as he sat down on the edge.

Leaning over her, he called to her softly.

"Betsy?"

* * *

Betsy heard a voice calling from far away; a voice she didn't recognize. Papa? Jack? No. neither of those. It was a deep baritone voice, and its gentleness made her feel safe. Sleepily she became aware of her surroundings, and barely opened her eyes enough to see Thad's tall frame leaning over her.

So, it was Thad, her husband.

Wait. Her *husband?*

Her eyes flew open, and suddenly she bolted out of bed to the other side.

"Oh," she said, with sudden realization. "Oh God, I have a *husband.*"

"Yes, you do," said Thad. "And I believe you promised to come to me when I call you."

She blinked, and her eyelids drooped and threatened to close. When she opened them again suddenly, she gulped.

"But you haven't," she said, "yet."

Thad crooked a finger at her. "Come here, Elizabeth. I want to ask you something."

She stared at him as he patted the side of the bed. "You could ask me from *there*," she answered, her voice full of suspicion.

The side of his mouth lifted. "I *will* ask you from here. And you're going to be sitting right beside me. Come to me. *Now*."

Betsy felt her eyes widen. He was serious.

"And if I don't?"

"We've discussed that already, and I told you what would happen if you don't. I'm waiting."

His smile was gone now. Betsy gauged the distance to the door, and he shook his head.

"Don't even think about trying to run. You won't succeed. You're making this harder than you need to, sweetheart. I just want to talk to you."

She licked her lips nervously. "Are the guests still here?"

"They're gone," he said, "and *you're* stalling."

"Evie too?"

"Left for the day. It's just you and me, Elizabeth. She'll be back in the morning. She's willing to help you go through the boxes and help you put away your things." His voice lowered as he next spoke. "And I'm *still* waiting."

She sighed. "I... can't seem to get my feet to move."

"Shall I come and get you?"

She looked away, knowing fear was on her face. As he rose, she realized again just how tall he was, and took a deep breath.

"You need not fear me, young lady, but when I call you, I expect you to come."

"How... do I know for sure I shouldn't fear you?" Her eyes widened as she watched him approach her, around the bed.

"I suppose you'll have to learn to trust me. I know that may take time, but I'll eventually prove it to you." He lifted her into his arms in one swift motion. In a few seconds, he sat down on the bed and placed her in his lap, embracing her gently but firmly.

Betsy glanced up into his face. "You said you wanted to ask me something."

"Yes. First, I wanted to ask you if your headache is better." Before she could answer, he added, "The truth, Elizabeth. I'll know if you're lying."

She lowered her gaze. "It's gone. Well, *mostly* gone."

He raised her chin to bring her eyes up to his again. "That's the truth?"

She nodded. "But I... guess you want to..."

"Yes. I do want to make love to you. But it can wait until tonight if you like. Although I refuse to wait any longer than that."

She could feel her face growing hot, and she knew it was must be scarlet.

"Are you hungry?" He traced her cheek with his finger. "You haven't eaten since noon, and Evaline left us some supper."

Slowly, she nodded. "I would like that."

He set her on the floor and rose, taking her hand. "Then let's find something to eat."

* * *

Evie had left them a cozy little meal, including fresh bread and cheese and a big bowl of chicken and dumplings. She'd also left them each a large piece of the wedding cake, with a note that said, "I knew you wouldn't have time to eat any, so I saved it for you."

Betsy smiled at Evie's thoughtfulness as she helped set the food out on the table and sat next to him. She noticed Thad watching her as they sat silently through the meal.

Finally, he leaned toward her. "Talk to me, sweetheart."

She glanced up with wariness. It was not the first time he'd called her that.

Thad gave her a smile. "Yes. You *are* a sweetheart. And you're adorable. Do you realize that? Tell me about your past. I want to know who you are. Where are you really from? And so, help me, if you say Philadelphia—"

She cut him off with a laugh. "I'm from Castle's Woods, Virginia. But my grandmother was from Philadelphia. She never forgave Papa for marrying my mother and taking her away from home. She wasn't a Blankenship, though, or a Raine, or any of the other names they asked about. My father was a Lawrence from Castle's Woods. Does that satisfy you?"

He eyed her, grinning. "That's the truth?"

Mischievous dimples creased her cheeks. "It's the truth. And who are *you*?"

"I'm originally from New Haven. I've lived out here for years, long before Fort John became Fort Laramie. I helped to negotiate the treaty last year between the Sioux and the Blackfoot and Crow, and the Arapaho and Cheyenne, and some others. The Indians trust me because they know I have their best interests at heart. This was originally their land, after all. The men from the government trust me too. I try to keep them both happy." He paused, frowning. "It's difficult, and I want you to understand there may be times I have to leave suddenly and be gone for periods of time."

Betsy set her fork down. "Will you be in danger?"

He studied her face thoughtfully. "Perhaps. But you mustn't worry about it."

Her shoulders fell, and her voice was incredulous. "How can I keep from worrying? You are my husband, after all."

He bent to kiss her mouth. "There is one thing you can do to make me happy. Make our time pleasant while I'm home." The kiss was gentle, and he glanced down at her plate. "Are you finished eating?"

She glanced down at the unfinished food on her plate. "I suppose so. Why?"

"Because I want to take you to my bed and ravish you."

Betsy felt her eyes grow wide.

"You *did* ask," he said."

She looked away. "Good Lord. I must remember not to do that."

His laughter filled the room, and he reached for her. Betsy pushed away from the table with the intention of running. But she was too late. His arm was around her waist before she got out of the chair.

For the second time that day, she found herself thrown over his shoulder.

"Oh, *no* you don't. I'm learning your ways, young lady. And while you're learning *mine*, you might try remembering not to run from me when you know I want you. I know you're fast, but I'm faster than you, and I'll catch you, just as I did earlier today outside the fort. Trust me." His hand slid up under her gown, and a second later he had thrown her dress upward. His hand came down, hard, on her bottom in a forcible slap.

She let out a whimper as he sat down on the bed and put her over his thigh.

He paused, and bent over her. "Did you mean it when you said you would love, honor and obey me?"

She sniffled. "Does it matter?"

Thad looked down at the young woman he'd placed face down over his lap. Her hair was tousled, and he'd raised her skirts until her heart-shaped bottom was visible. He turned her slightly so he could see her face. Tears were shimmering on her lashes, and she was trying to wipe them away.

Her question touched him. Did she really think her words and actions didn't matter to him?

Easing her over on her back, he leaned farther over her.

"Of course, it matters. I want you to be happy, Elizabeth."

Another whimper escaped, and she choked out a sob. "Then you might begin by letting me go."

Thad shook his head, and lifted her into his arms, cradling her. "Listen to me, sweetheart. I want to make love to you, but I also want you to be willing. I'm not going to force you. And right now, I think it would be best if you came to me and asked for it. I'll help you out of your wedding gown and into your nightgown. You do have one?"

She looked surprised. "I... yes, but I don't know where it is right now."

"Then I'll undress you and hold you next to me until you sleep."

She gasped. "Not *naked*!"

Thad tilted her chin upward. "I am your husband. Remember?"

She lowered her eyes, and he lifted her until she was sitting on his lap, turned away from him. "Sit still. I'll undo your buttons. There is no way you could have fastened all these buttons yourself."

"Suzy fastened them for me." The words sounded dejected, and they were followed by a hiccup. Thad was glad she couldn't see his smile. She had no idea just how adorable she was.

Slowly, he unfastened the buttons one at a time, and helped her off with the gown. The undergarments came next, until the pile of them lay over the chair in the corner. Then he held the coverlet and the sheets out in the big bed for her to crawl into. She met his eyes warily as he covered her up to her chin and tucked her in. He also noticed she was shivering.

"I'll secure the house, and then I'll be back. The heat from my body will warm you."

When he returned, she was turned on her left side, away from him, and appeared to be sleeping. She had scooted all the way over to the edge of the bed, and he knew if she moved any closer to it, she'd fall over the side.

Discarding his own garments, he climbed into bed beside her and pulled her closer against him.

"Sleep, sweetheart," he whispered into her ear.

She gave off a soft little sigh. It was the last thing he heard from her.

Betsy wasn't asleep. Her mind was busy. She was relieved he had decided to let her sleep rather than forcing her, but she was a little disappointed, too. She'd heard from her friends back home, how making love made a woman feel. Cherished. Protected. Needed. *Cared* for.

Could it be so? Her mother had never discussed the act of the wedding night with her, but her married friends had, long before she'd left home.

Before she'd reached her twentieth birthday, she'd decided no one was ever going to want her. Now, here she was, naked and in bed with her husband, and he didn't seem to want her either.

She remembered what he'd said when she asked him this morning. "Are you sure you want *me*?"

He'd said *no*. Was she so unlovable that he couldn't stand the thought of carrying through with it? He'd fully admitted it was an arrangement. She shouldn't be surprised he didn't want her. She held it in as long as she could. Eventually, however, her willpower gave way, and her shoulders shook with silent sobs of rejection.

She felt his arms tighten around her.

"Betsy? What is it? The truth, please."

She couldn't help it. She let out a sob. "You—*don't* want me," she wailed.

He turned her in bed to face him. "Whatever makes you think that?" he demanded. "Tell me *now*."

"You said you expected me to be in your bed at night but now you don't want me."

"I do want you, but you tried to run from me when I reached for you. What I *don't* want is to force you into something you fear. You've been through a lot. The last thing I want to do is to rob you of the one thing you have left, against your will. Your virginity." He stared down at her. "Or," he whispered in a growl, "perhaps it's *not* against your will?"

She shook her head, slowly, and his voice seemed to change.

"You give your consent, then?"

A nod. "But not—*not* if you don't want me."

She heard the smile in his voice when he spoke. "Oh, my little sweetheart. You've *no* idea."

Thad caged her in with his arms as he stared down at her. The small face he peered down into looked up with a hopeful expression. In response, he lowered his mouth to hers, kissing her hard, then again. And *again*. He traced those luscious lips with his tongue, and heard her sharp intake of breath before sweeping powerfully inward.

Under him, Betsy stilled, and he gentled his touch. She'd likely never done this before, and he wanted to be careful with her. His tongue moved inside her mouth, and she moaned with pleasure.

"You're a darling," he said softly, into her mouth. When she whimpered, he added, "and you're *my* darling. I feel as if I'm a very lucky man."

"Really?"

"I don't say things I don't mean, sweetheart. You'll learn that quite quickly."

Betsy's eyes widened, and he smiled.

"By the time I'm finished with you, I hope you'll know you're cherished."

She looked up, as if she couldn't believe what he was saying. "Cherished?"

"Yes, sweetheart. *Cherished*."

Later...

She lay there, in the circle of his arms, as he drew her closer to him. He had loved her mercilessly, and their marriage was consummated and complete as he held her next to him. She had reached her peak several times before he did. And she knew her girlfriends had been right. It was beautiful, and she felt protected, needed, cared for, and yes, cherished.

"Yes," she whispered softly. "Cherished."

Chapter Four

U *nexpected times...*

Thad awakened her the next morning, bringing kisses to her face, and she opened her eyes. The light in the room was growing, and she smiled.

"Do you want me again?"

"Oh yes," he growled into her ear, "but I hear Evaline in the kitchen making breakfast, so I suppose we'll need to get up and eat. Lovemaking will have to wait until tonight." He smiled at the look of disappointment on her face, and kissed her, hard.

"Patience, sweetheart. Hopefully I'll see you at noon."

"Thad? I don't have anything to wear. All my things are soiled."

He stared at her briefly before moving to the hearth and bringing the fire back to life. Then, turning to the chest and opening it, he pulled out a long nightshirt and brought it to the bed.

"Here. Stand up."

"What?"

"You heard me. Stand up. This may be long on you but it'll have to do."

Betsy shyly scooted over to his side of the bed and stood, squealing when he pulled the blanket away from her in the cool room. Wrapping her in the wool nightshirt, he ignored her protests that it was scratchy, and fastened the buttons.

"I'll have Evaline find you something else as soon as possible, but you can wear this until then."

"You're so thoughtful," she said, with distinct sarcasm.

In answer, his hand connected with her bottom in a playful swat, and she squealed.

"Be nice, my love. We'll get you in something suitable to wear today. I promise."

Betsy returned his glance less than enthusiastically, but remained silent as he led her into the kitchen. Evaline was busy making breakfast.

"Good morning," she said cheerfully.

"Morning," Thad grinned. "Can you help Betsy find some of her clothes today and help her launder them?"

Evie turned to see the shirt he had put on Betsy. "Oh my. Instead of that scratchy thing? Of course. First thing. There is already water boiling on the stove."

"Thank you, Miss Evie," Betsy added. "I would so appreciate it."

"Just Evie." The answer came quickly. "I haven't been a miss in many years now."

Betsy glanced at Thad, who smiled back at her. "Evaline's husband passed a few years ago," he said softly.

"Yes, and I miss him every single day," the woman said quietly to Betsy, adding, "I hope you're hungry. This is a big breakfast."

"Yes, ma'am. I'm starved. And it looks delicious."

"Good, because if we manage to get your washing all caught up it'll be a long day. We'll put on some beans and cornbread to cook for supper while we work. It looks as if we've a bundle of things to go through today."

* * *

Betsy was aware of Thad's gaze on her as she tried not to scratch her way through breakfast wearing the wool shirt. Finally, he gave up and took her back into the bedroom.

"You're uncomfortable," he said. "I didn't realize how much wool would bother you. Here." He pulled out a cotton shirt from the wardrobe. "Put this on instead. It won't be as warm, but at least it will cover you."

Betsy took it with a grateful smile and Thad brought the wool garment off over her head, examining her skin in the lamplight.

"I was thinking of keeping you warm. I didn't know you'd react so much to it. Sorry, sweetheart."

When she continued glaring at him, he shook his head. "Why didn't you tell me?"

"I didn't think it would matter."

"For pity's sake, of course it would matter. I have no desire to intentionally make you suffer. You must think me a barbarian." He took her into his arms and lifted her chin so her mouth was next to his, kissing her in a way that made her knees weak. "I'm tempted to take you back to bed."

"Patience, sir. Hopefully, I'll see you at noon," she said mischievously, using the very words he'd spoken earlier.

He raised a brow. "A warning, sweetheart. Using my words against me will get you into trouble."

"Oh?"

He turned her to face away from him and swatted her bottom. "Yes. Behave yourself, and get dressed. You'll have a lot to attend to today. Hear?"

"Yes." She scowled at him, and pulled on the cotton shirt he'd given her. The sleeves hung down well below her fingertips, and she stood patiently while Thad rolled them up. "This is much better," she said.

He bent to kiss her forehead. "Be a good girl today."

With that, he left the room.

* * *

Betsy wandered back into the kitchen to find Evie busily clearing the table and washing dishes. She paused, when she saw the cotton shirt, and let out a chuckle.

"I knew he wouldn't make you wear the wool all day."

"I'll be so glad to get some of my own clothes on," Betsy murmured.

"And it won't be long. The water is in the tub now, and the soap is ready. We can get busy washing."

They began the day by going into the back room where the things were stored and opening crates. Recognizing some of them, Betsy helped to move them around and began by pulling out clothes of her own.

Evie looked up, smiling. "There is only one wash-board," she lamented, "but we'll do the best we can. The beans are cooking on the stove, and there's more water heating."

By seven they had begun washing, and by ten, many of her clothes were hanging on the line in the back, blowing in the breeze as they dried.

"Thank you, Miss—" she caught herself. "Thank you, Evie, so much for your help."

Evie smiled. "When I was a new bride, I didn't know how to do anything. We had servants at home, so I wasn't allowed to help. I realize you know how to wash clothes, but I also know you can use some help. If there's anything you need me to show you, please ask."

"I was wondering," Betsy paused, and then shook her head. What she wanted to know was none of her business.

"Speak your mind and feel free, Betsy. You were wondering why I didn't go back home after my husband died?"

Betsy gulped. "Yes. How did you know?"

"Your face is easy to read, child. I'll answer. I didn't

think I'd be welcome at home if I tried to return. My parents were completely opposed to me marrying a soldier. When we married despite their wishes, they not only expressed their displeasure, they took my name off the will. Even if they'd changed their minds after that, I wouldn't have gone back. Besides," she smiled, "I have friends here. When my husband died, Thad knew I needed work. He offered me house-keeping and doing chores here a few days a week. I chose three days each week, because it would give me enough pay to stay here. The house I live in isn't mine, but the captain said I could continue to live in it as long as I wanted. Your Thad made it possible for me to stay. He's a good man, Betsy."

"So everyone keeps telling me," Betsy sighed.

Evie smiled. "You'll find it to be true, too, once you know him better."

"I hope so."

The smile on Evie's face grew. "You will. Trust me. Here. Let me go outside and check on your clothes. They may be dry by now. I'm sure your underthings are."

"Thank you, Evie. I do know how to iron if you need me to."

As Evie left, Betsy leaned back on her heels and studied the remaining crates. The labels were on the side next to the wall, making it impossible to tell what was in them. She reached for the one nearest her, lifting the top upward.

Her mother's favorite blue gingham frock was lying on the top. Betsy recoiled as if it was a snake and dropped the lid. Memories, one after the other of Mama and Papa rose in her mind. Papa teaching her to ride... Mama's praise when Betsy made her first apron with pockets on it... The surprise on Papa's face when she'd beat him at poker for the first time.

It hit her suddenly. She hadn't really had the chance to say goodbye, nor had she been able to mourn their loss. The desire to run away and hide, and do nothing but sob her heart out was strong.

When Evie returned, Betsy was in a heap on the floor, weeping uncontrollably.

"My—mother's... things," she choked out.

"Oh, Betsy," Evie's arms engulfed her, suddenly. "I'm so sorry. We don't have to do these today if you'd rather not."

Betsy shook her head, but couldn't stop the tears from escaping. "I-I need to get these finished and out of the way. I can't let my past take up a room in Thad's house forever."

"It's not just my house. It's *our* house, Elizabeth."

A soft male voice from the doorway caused her to look up suddenly.

Betsy was surprised to see Thad standing there, concern on his face. He moved past Evie and knelt down beside her, lifting her up and carrying her out of the room.

"Shh, and don't you dare apologize. I wondered when you'd finally break down and cry. You're tough, aren't you? But even tough little girls need time to grieve."

Betsy didn't answer, and Thad laid down on the bed with her wrapped in his arms.

"Now, sweetheart. Cry it out."

His permission to grieve opened the floodgates, and she wept for what seemed hours. How unfair could life be, to take her parents from her and then make her marry a man she barely knew? She'd given up her life in Castle's Woods, a place she'd loved. She'd recognized, however, that look in her father's eyes when he began planning the trip to the west. He was determined to go; he was *eager* to go. If she wanted to keep her parents in her life, she knew it was necessary to go with them.

And then... *then*, she'd lost them.

Fate must be laughing at her recent twist of events.

At the end, she'd been forced to start a new life; so far, one she wasn't sure she could adjust to.

No. That's not entirely true. I was forced to start a new life the day I left on the wagon train.

A wave of fresh tears struck as she realized she'd never see home or family again. But as her weary lids began to droop, she realized Thad was rocking her gently in his arms and whispering to her.

"Shh, Betsy. I have you now," he said softly.

Betsy finally quieted in his arms. They were so comforting;

"Thad? Please hold me?" she whispered into his neck.

"Always, sweetheart. Always."

An hour later, she opened her eyes. She'd been asleep?

Pushing herself up, she glanced around the room. The wardrobe door had been left open, and her clean frock of pale blue hung in it, along with her chemise, her petticoats, and her corset.

She sighed and sat up straight. She couldn't stay in the bedroom all day, and if she *didn't* come out, Evie would sit in the back room and keep washing it all, alone.

With a saddened sigh, she rose and began to dress. The chemise went on first, but the corset, she stared at with distaste. Finally, she stuffed it in the bottom of the wardrobe. When the gown was fastened, she worked her hair into a long braid, as she'd worn it during the journey. The inside door of the wardrobe had a long mirror attached; she noticed it as she tied a matching ribbon at the end.

When she came back into the kitchen, Evie was working on lunch. Wonderful aromas were coming from the room, and Betsy felt guilty for leaving her to do all the work alone.

"I... apologize," she said humbly, as she entered, "for leaving you."

Evie only smiled. "This is my job, Betsy. I'm paid to do the cooking."

"But you weren't paid to go through all my things and wash them."

Evie turned to face her. "No," she said. "I'm not. I did that because I wanted to. Don't allow yourself any guilt, honey, because of what I do for you. It's my joy to help you."

Betsy threw her arms about the woman's neck. "Thank you, ma'am."

Evie threw her head back, laughing. "And don't call me ma'am. I feel old enough as it is. All right?"

They both turned as a thunderous pounding was heard on the front door. Evaline frowned.

"I wonder who that could be?"

"I'll get it," Betsy offered. Moving toward the front room, she opened it a crack.

And gasped.

An Indian warrior stood outside the door, the look on his face dark and forbidding.

"Pardon?" she spoke meekly, taking a step back.

It was a mistake. As she moved back, he took hold of the door and moved inside.

"Chief's son sick."

"I'm sorry. My husband isn't home and I—" She could have kicked herself the moment the words left her mouth.

Was that a pleased expression on his face?

"Come. Need you."

"Wait. I'm not a nurse..." But he had already grabbed hold of her upper arm and was pulling her toward the horses tied at the post outside.

"Quick," he said.

Betsy tried to tug free of his grasp. "Wait--who *are* you?"

He stood straight, looking down at her. "Name Akecheta. Warrior."

Betsy didn't doubt it. He *looked* like a warrior.

"Atech..." she tried to repeat it, but was unable. "Evie!" she called out, hoping the housekeeper was nearby, but the warrior had already closed the door behind them. He dragged her to the horse; hands grabbed her by the waist, and put her on its back before she could get away.

How long would it be before Evie realized she was gone?

The warrior shouted commands to the horses; hers followed his to the gates. There were two soldiers guarding it, and Betsy tried to motion to them for help. But their eyes seemed to rest only on the warrior, not on her. Before she knew it, they were on the outside. One of the soldiers saw her and seemed to take note of her plea for help before a roar from the warrior turned her attention back to him. She held tightly onto the mane of the horse and leaned forward, hoping to keep from falling off.

Betsy knew her eyes were wide. Was he really taking her to the chief? She didn't trust him, not one bit. Another thought occurred to her. What if he was, and she was unable to help the child? Would they kill her if she couldn't help?

He guided them at a gallop down beside the river. As they rounded the corner of the fort, they passed a group of men standing in a huddle several hundred yards away. They were dressed much as the warrior in front of her. They eyed her suspiciously as she passed, murmuring among themselves. Two of them broke away from the group and mounted their horses, riding away quickly in the opposite direction.

What was happening? Betsy remained quiet. She was tempted to bring both legs over the horse's back and jump, and just about to do it when she heard thunderous hooves approaching from behind her. A large band of warriors surrounded them. Shouts filled the air, and bows and arrows were prepared to shoot from all sides.

Betsy was terrified as the man who had come for her galloped away, leaving her there in the midst of the shouts and the threats.

She felt her chest tighten, swearing to herself she'd never leave the fort again, for any reason. If Thad wanted to stay at his house outside the fort, he could do it *alone*.

She looked around at the warriors. They had put their arrows into their quivers, and were putting their bows away.

An older man among them approached her slowly. "Akecheta try take you hostage. Come. We take you to chief."

"But—that's where *he* said he was taking me."

"We send for White Panther to come for you."

Betsy stared at him. It occurred to her White Panther might be Thad, however he hadn't told her that. Almost, she believed the warrior. He didn't wait for her consent. The commands he issued sounded very like the ones Akecheta had made. Her horse followed obediently, and she held on, her hair loose now and flying out behind her in the wind.

Up ahead there was a group of teepees surrounded by men and women who were waiting in the distance. She hadn't quite reached it when the sound of a horse galloping closer was heard. A shout accompanied it. She turned to look back.

Thad was approaching, and fast.

The warriors around her slowed, and so did her horse. Her shoulders sagged with relief, until Thad was close enough to see his face. His expression was angry and forbidding, and Betsy couldn't take her eyes from him.

He slowed his horse even more, and as he came close enough, leaned over and transferred her to his own horse in front of him. His arm was tight around her waist. She tried to look up into his face, but he spoke quietly in her ear.

"We're going in, Elizabeth. Don't speak unless you're spoken to."

With a very slight nod, she agreed.

Thad kept the horse at a slow trot now as he approached the large tent in front of them. He tipped his hat toward the ladies who were smiling now, and Betsy wondered if he knew them.

When he stopped his mount, he slid to the ground and turned to reach for her. Taking hold of her waist, he brought her down next to him.

"Thad, are you sure this is a good idea—" she halted and bit her lip as he turned and gave her a stern look. She'd agreed to remain quiet until spoken to, and already, she'd forgotten her promise.

The flap to the tent was flung open, and a man in full Indian dress stood just inside. When he saw Thad, he nodded.

"Thad. Come."

"Chief Kohanawamblee. Good to see you. May I bring my bride?"

The man before them was the chief? Betsy stared at him with wide eyes.

He gave a nod. "Bring."

Betsy glanced at Thad warily. How was she to respond?

Thad answered by bending down and saying in a soft voice. "Nod, Elizabeth."

She hesitantly gave a slight bow, and let Thad lead her into the large tent.

It appeared even bigger from the inside. A woman was standing at the far edge, crooning to an infant in her arms who was whimpering. As the chief stared back at the child, worry knit his brow.

So, Akecheta was right, and this must be the sick child.

Betsy continued to watch as a moment later the Chief concentrated his gaze on them. He spoke, but it was in his own tongue, and she understood nothing. Then he became quiet, and Thad answered.

Betsy continued to watch the chief's face. A furrow had crossed his brow, indicating he was disturbed. He spoke once more, and Thad turned to face her, taking her hands in his.

"Tell me," he commanded softly. "What happened?"

Betsy kept her eyes on him as she explained what had taken place. But when he repeated it to the chief, the man squinted toward her.

"Son *is* sick," he said, "but not send for *you*. Akecheta try before to make trouble between Sioux and White Man." He turned to Thad. "We take care of him. He do this *last time*."

The rest of the conversation was in Sioux, and

Betsy willingly leaned into her husband, relaxing slightly for a while. As her concentration waned, however, she glanced around the tent.

The woman carrying the infant was watching her, and their eyes met.

Betsy hardly realized what she was doing as she left Thad's side and slowly approached the beautiful woman. In Indian dress, she moved forward, lifting one hand and motioning to her chest.

"Wachiwi," she said, motioning to herself. Then, she nodded toward the baby. "Wapi," she whispered.

Betsy smiled back at her. "Betsy," she said, motioning to herself before reaching out to touch the infant's tiny hand. "He's beautiful."

As if she understood, Wachiwi smiled back. Suddenly, Betsy realized the tiny boy had grasped a hand around her little finger, and she let out a small chuckle.

The chief turned and spoke to Thad in the Sioux tongue. Thad, realizing his wife had wandered to the other side of the tent, appeared grim. Betsy wondered if she'd made a grave mistake by approaching the baby. But as she tried to withdraw her hand from the infant's grasp, he held on tighter, unwilling to let go.

The chief's expression changed, suddenly as he watched, and his face broke into a smile. Thad's shoulders seemed to relax, but he motioned Betsy to come to him. Wachiwi managed to disengage the infant's hold on her finger, and Betsy gave a slight bow and moved back to her husband.

Thad reached for her and held her closely to his side as they said their goodbyes. He prepared to guide her back to his horse. But as they left the tent, the chief stopped them.

"Wife. Name?" He was pointing to her, and she stared at him silently. Thad nodded, indicating she should answer.

"Betsy," she said with a tremulous voice.

A wide smile spread across the chief's face. "Betsy... Bride of White Panther. Welcome. Always."

"Thank you, sir," she whispered.

He nodded, then turned to Thad. "Warriors take you back," the chief said firmly from the opening of his tent.

"Thank you, Swift Eagle. We would both appreciate that."

"What did you call him? I mean, when we first entered the tent?" Betsy whispered as they approached the opening of the fort once again.

"It's the meaning of his name in Sioux. Kohonawamblee means Swift Eagle. He's given me permission to use that name. Quiet, until I get you to the house." He turned to the warriors who had accompanied them and bowed before speaking in Sioux to them in a polite tone. They gave him a bow as well, and turned to ride home.

Thad stopped again just at the gates. "Elizabeth, were these the soldiers who were here when you were taken outside the gates?"

She nodded. Thad eyed them a moment, before taking her through it and toward the house.

They had almost reached it when the captain hailed them from his horse. "Suzy saw Akecheta taking her, but not before she could reach me to stop him.

"And the soldiers at the gate stood right there and *let* him?" Thad added.

Andrew nodded. "I'll take care of it. They're new, but that's no excuse."

"No. It isn't." Thad slid to the ground and reined the horse before lifting Betsy down. "Into the house, Elizabeth. And bolt the doors, front and back until I return."

Betsy opened her mouth to speak, but when she saw his face, she closed it again and went inside. Looking back through the window, she watched as he and Andrew exchanged a heated debate, and Andrew motioned him to follow. Both disappeared toward a stucco building with a sign on the front.

"Bolt the door." Evie's whispered voice brought her to the present.

"Oh! He did say that." She moved quickly to comply.

"Betsy, I'm so sorry. When I realized you weren't coming back, I looked out the front window and didn't see you anywhere. I had no idea where you'd gone. What happened?"

Betsy sighed and moved into the kitchen, plopping down into a chair at the table. Repeating the story to Evie from start to finish, Betsy couldn't help but notice the frightened look on Evie's face. The story was barely finished when they heard pounding on the front door. This time Evie motioned her to stay.

"It'll be Thad. I'll get it."

Chapter Five

E *xplaining...*

Betsy didn't take her eyes off her husband when he made his way into the kitchen. He appeared at his wit's end. "Andrew's too lenient," he said furiously. "If it were me, I'd have dealt far worse with them for letting this happen. I made it clear to them in no uncertain terms that you were never to be allowed outside the gates without me. And that Akecheta was never to be allowed *inside*. But I'm not sure they were listening." He turned to Betsy. "I'm sure you're full of questions, sweetheart. Go ahead and ask."

Betsy nodded, taking a deep breath.

"What's wrong with the baby?"

Thad stared at her.

"The chief's son?"

"Yes. He looks like he hasn't been fed in days."

Thad pulled out a chair directly in front of her and sat down, taking her hands in his. "He needs goat's milk. And there isn't another woman in the tribe right now who can be a wet nurse to him. His mother has no milk."

"Then let's find him a goat."

Thad shook his head. "Sweetheart, there was a plague of anthrax throughout the livestock in the area not long ago. The goat population has all but disappeared and he can't digest cow's milk."

Betsy stood and began to pace. Suddenly she turned back.

"You said '*all* but disappeared.'"

"Yes."

"There must be someone who has some, then?"

He reached for her hand. "Sit down, sweetheart. There is one rancher in the territory who wasn't affected. His name is Henry Lake. We've tried to talk him into selling some of his milk. He's vehemently refused. We've tried to talk him into selling one of the goats. Joseph the Longhunter almost managed, but when Henry realized it was to feed the son of one of the Indians, he refused."

"Why?"

"Because he has a hatred for the Indian, regardless the tribe."

Betsy eyed him incredulously. "What if *I* asked?"

He tugged her down into the seat, eyeing her suspiciously. "Absolutely *not*. You aren't to go anywhere near him. He's a cruel man, Elizabeth. One of the warriors even tried to steal one, but it did not go well, and it's been the source of much of the conflict we've had recently."

"But—" She halted abruptly when he leaned close enough to be inches from her face.

"I said no. That means *no*. And don't ask me to change my mind, because I won't."

Betsy sighed, giving up for the moment.

"All right. Then I have another question. What did the chief say today when we were there and he was talking to you in his own language?"

He softened, leaning back, and began to explain.

Betsy listened attentively. "And what did he mean when he came to the door of the tent as we left? He said, 'Welcome'."

"He meant you would always be welcome to the tribe. What he was saying, sweetheart, was that you were trusted, and he knew you would never betray that trust."

Betsy was touched. She met his gaze with misty eyes. "I'm honored," she whispered.

Thad leaned forward and planted a kiss on her nose. "What else do you want to know?"

"You said you spoke to the soldiers at the gate. What happened to them? Did the captain let them go back to work?"

"They're both in the brig. And Andrew put out orders for Akecheta never to come inside the gates again."

Betsy scowled. "The brig? I don't think it was a severe enough offense to do *that*."

He continued staring at her. "You don't, eh?"

"No," she said firmly, "I don't."

He took her shoulders and raised her to her feet, leading her toward the bedroom. "Let me explain some things to you, young lady."

Betsy sighed as he led her inside and pulled her down on the edge of the bed next to him. He was going to *explain*, whether she liked it or not.

Betsy was staring back at him with eyes the size of saucers when he finished explaining what might have happened to her had someone been allowed to take her as hostage.

She gasped. "Oh, Thad. I didn't know."

"Well, the Sioux warriors who have loyalty to Swift Eagle *did*. Now, do you understand why I'm so upset the soldiers let it happen?"

She moved to him, putting her arms around him as far as she could. "I understand. I can't thank you enough for coming after me. I didn't know what was to become of me."

"Swift Eagle's warriors would have kept you safe until I got there. But if they hadn't been there to see you..." His arms were around her tightly, and he tucked her head under his chin. "Dear God, Elizabeth. *Anyone* could have taken you. When I think what could have happened..."

"But it didn't, Thad. It *didn't*. I'm all right, and I'll be so careful from now on."

His eyes were closed when she looked up into his face, and she raised up on tiptoe to kiss his cheek.

"Thank you," she whispered, "for coming to my rescue."

When he opened one eye and raised a brow, his voice was humble. "This is partly my fault. I should have warned you yesterday not to go outside the gates. It's too dangerous for you. If someone tries to do it again, you're to begin screaming as soon as you're taken from the front door"

"I will. I promise. But I have a question. Would you explain what kinds of problems there are between Akecheta and the chief? They're both Sioux, aren't they?"

He didn't answer for several seconds. When he finally spoke, his voice was quiet. "Betsy, you're asking things I shouldn't be discussing. One thing I've learned over the years? *Don't meddle in a tribe's affairs when it doesn't concern you.* Swift Eagle said he'll take care of it. But if he does, there may be war within the tribe. Neither of them want that. The Sioux keep their dwellings further out, and the Chief's warriors keep a close eye on their surroundings. That's why they spotted him while he was still the only one with you. They got to him first."

Betsy scowled. "So I can't go outside? Am I to be kept prisoner in my own house, then?"

"Wait a few days, sweetheart, and let's see what happens. If he stays away, it may be all right to let you leave the house as long as you stay inside the fort. Susannah runs about freely, but she carries a pistol with her, and Andrew has made sure she's a good shot."

When she didn't answer, he moved his hands to her shoulders and sat down on the bed, pulling her down next to him. "Now it's my turn to ask *you* something. Tell me, what do you need in order to make the upstairs into a complete sewing room?"

"You're changing the topic of conversation."

"I realize that, but I need to know."

"I think I have everything I need except a cutting table," she responded softly. "The other things are all among my mother's crates in the back room. I just need to finish searching through them until I find what I need."

"If I can find you a table," he answered, "can you keep busy up there for a few days until we see what will happen?"

Betsy observed his face. It was full of concern, and she smiled. "I'm sure I can. But Thad, the chief's baby... He looks very sick."

"I know, sweetheart. I *know*. Give us a few more days to work on it, all right?"

"But he may not *have* a few more days," she protested. "This is so unfair."

"You didn't answer my question."

She stared at him defiantly. "Well, I wouldn't like to have to be imprisoned up here forever."

A smile crept across his handsome mouth. "You won't be, I promise. I have some things to take care of this afternoon, but this evening, I'll carry the heavy things up to your room." He bent to plant a brief kiss on her forehead. "See what you and Evaline can find this afternoon."

"Could I..." Betsy licked her lips, "work on making some curtains for the windows downstairs?"

"Downstairs?" he echoed. "Don't you need some upstairs, too? I'd rather people not be able to see you through the windows up here working."

"Yes, but..."

"Ah. I understand. You don't *care* for the ones downstairs."

She looked away. "Well..."

Thad grinned. "The truth? I don't care much for them, either. Sure. Do I need to take you to the Trading Post to find the goods?"

She shook her head. "I think I may have several yards of material among my mother's things."

"All right. But if you need more, let me know."

She flashed him a smile, and nodded. "I will."

Thad lifted her chin for a brief kiss, and reminded her to bolt the door behind him as he left. He waited outside until he heard the sound of it before leaving. She was being more compliant than he'd expected, and that unnerved him. He wasn't sure if it was due to her relief at being rescued, or gratefulness she wasn't in trouble, but either way, he was glad. Or, could it possibly be that she was planning something? He didn't know. But if he could keep her busy and inside for the next few days with Evaline, he'd be thankful.

Perhaps he could have Suzy visit too, to bring the outside world to her, since Betsy couldn't go to *it*.

He turned to look back toward the house. Her small face peeked back at him from the window, and he gave her a wink.

She smiled just before she disappeared from view.

Betsy wandered back into the kitchen where she found Evie busy preparing dinner.

"I have most of the housework done for the day. Just getting started on supper. Would you like to go into the back room and sort through the crates again?"

"I'd love it. I asked Thad if I could make some curtains for the downstairs windows. Somewhere in all those crates are some goods that would make really nice curtains."

Evie grinned. "Then let's go look."

A moment later, they were moving and sorting things into stacks. Betsy felt proud of herself for being able to look through them without falling apart. Her mother's garments went into one stack; her father's into another.

Evie rested one hand on her mother's things. "Betsy, we could alter these to make them suitable for you, but it would be a challenge."

Betsy's face was doubtful. "I have plenty of things that fit," she said softly. "Now they're all clean, I'll be set. Perhaps someone else could use them? She glanced at Evie. "What about you? Would they fit you?"

A smile lit Evie's face. "They're very well made, and I could use some clothes right now."

"Then they're yours. Take them."

"Oh, Betsy, are you sure? I could work a day or two extra for the next few weeks to pay you for them—"

"Oh, no ma'am. It's a gift. Mother was tall, like you, and she'd be thrilled for you to have them. Just *take* them."

Evie reached for the one on the top, holding it up next to her. Her eyes were shining, and Betsy reached underneath the stack and handed the whole thing to her.

But Evie held up a hand. "Wait. Are you sure it won't bother you to see me wearing her things?"

"I think it would be a comfort to see you in them. And I know she would want you to have them."

The expression on the housekeeper's face was suddenly unreadable. Betsy wondered if she'd made a mistake, when tears began trailing their way down Evie's cheeks.

"Oh, Betsy," she whispered softly. "I can't thank you enough."

"All right, then. Consider it a trade?" Betsy said. "Sewing is the only thing I do well. Consider it a payment for all the teaching you'll give me about cooking and housekeeping?"

Evie put out a hand. "It's done."

A laugh escaped, and Betsy reached for another stack of clothes, this time her father's.

"Now, about these. They might fit Thad, but I think it truly would bother me to see him wearing them. And I'd like to make him a few things. I was searching through the wardrobe, and it looks as if he could use a fall jacket. As soon as I can save up the money, I might visit the Trading Post. Do you know of any of the men in the fort who might use these things?"

Evie stared at them. "Most of the soldiers wear uniforms. Let me think about it? I do believe I might be able to find someone. The gentleman who runs the trading post has a brother who might be able to use some of them. And the man who runs the sawmill nearby. And the..."

They continued talking as they worked their way through the stacks of things. Before she realized it, Betsy had one of the empty crates full of things to send home with Evie. She promised to have Thad bring the rest; a few quilts to use, and some to give away. At the bottom of one of the crates, they found the goods Betsy sought for the downstairs curtains.

"Oh my," Evie fingered the material gently, admiring the design, "This is lovely. I think Thad will like it. Yellow is one of my favorite colors."

"I hope so. My mother saved up for the material before she and Papa decided to come west," Betsy explained. She thought she'd use it when we reached the coast."

"It's just perfect. Not too feminine and not too masculine."

* * *

They finished supper before Betsy explained that she was sending a crate home with Evie to distribute to a few people in the fort. Thad carried it to Evie's house, letting Betsy walk over between them.

As she approached, she managed to control her expressions. The place Evie lived was little more than a small hut, and although it showed recent repair, the inside was rather shabby. The curtains were faded and drab, and so were the covers for the furniture cushions. She remembered her father's advice to her, however, as a child.

"A poker game isn't the only time to put on a face that gives away nothing," he'd said. Vowing to herself to send more things home with Evie in the future, she kept the presence of a smile.

As they made their way home, hand in hand, Thad was quiet, and Betsy turned to him.

"What are you thinking?"

His returned glance was a frown. "This is the first time I've been inside Evaline's house. It needs some things, doesn't it? Andrew wasn't kidding when he said she was needing work in order to stay here. And you were kind to send some nice things home with her. I hope she can use some of them."

Betsy looked away. "Only a few things," she said quietly.

When she glanced back up at him, however, he was observing her face. Smiling, he brought her close to his side.

"My girl," he said softly.

* * *

Betsy admired her husband as he began carrying things upstairs for her. She showed him the material she planned to use for the curtains downstairs, but as he deposited it on the rocker upstairs in the sewing room, she frowned at it.

She knew why. Evie needed them, far more than she.

Thad bent down to her ear. "You're eyeing this material with distaste, sweetheart. Do you not like it?"

"No, it's not that. I *do* like it. It's just... Evie saw this material when we looked through the crates, and she really loved it, and..." she paused. "After seeing her house this evening, I think she needs it more than we do. This is lovely, and there's enough here to cover some cushions for her furniture too. It would make her cottage cheery and bright. Don't you think?"

His glance was curious. "You're thinking about giving it away?"

She sighed, and nodded. "How old do you think her furniture is?"

"I don't know. But I don't expect that's your concern. She's a proud woman, sweetheart. I've been careful what I've offered to her so far. But if your heart's set on it, you can think about how she would react to your offer, go ahead. I honestly don't know the answer."

She glanced up. "You said if I wanted, you would buy some goods to do the curtains for downstairs."

"True. Is that what you want?"

"It's what I want."

He tilted her chin upward. "You're sure."

"Yes."

"Then I'll take you tomorrow to the Trading Post and see what Joseph has. He has a catalogue, too. You can order from it if you like, although it would take a while for it to arrive."

"Only," she licked her lips thoughtfully, "don't tell anyone about it, all right?"

He grinned. "If you like."

"Yes!" She danced around, waving her arms with glee. Thad leaned against the frame of the doorway, grinning and shaking his head.

"You, sweetheart, are a delight," he said, finally.

Someone was pounding on the door downstairs, and he turned, frowning. "It seems we have company."

She watched as he descended the steps. "Now it's your turn to look distasteful."

"Well," he turned to glance back up at her. "I was hoping to have my new bride all to myself this evening." With a wink, he disappeared around the corner and from sight.

A moment later, Suzy's demanding voice echoed up the staircase. "Where *is* she?"

"In her sewing room. Be my guest."

Even though she couldn't see him, Betsy could imagine the half-smile on her husband's face as he answered.

"Quiet, Suz," Andrew's voice followed.

Suzy appeared a moment later. As she reached the top, she drew Betsy into her arms. "How are you? Are you all right? What did they do to you?"

Thad followed her up with a stool, and moved to the rocker, setting the material down next to it.

"Here. You two might as well sit," he said jovially. "This will take a while."

Susannah waited until he was gone before leaning forward. "Tell me."

* * *

Thad reached the first floor to find Andrew pacing, his hands jammed in his pockets.

"What's going on?"

Andrew turned to face him as he approached. "Suz has been tenacious. She's been demanding all afternoon that she be able to come over and see your wife for herself and make sure she's all right."

"If I'd known that I'd have stopped by. We just escorted Evaline home with a crate of things." He stopped, eyeing Andrew suspiciously. "Something's happened. What is it?"

Andrew lowered his voice, glancing at the stairwell. "Mose and James--the soldiers who were in the brig?"

Thad leaned forward. "Yes?"

"They overpowered the jailor. He's over at the doc's house, and he might not make it."

Alarm spread across Thad's face like wildfire. His own voice dropped an octave.

"And the soldiers?"

"They're *gone*."

Thad stared at him for a full minute, his mind whirling. "You need me to go with you." It was a statement, not a question.

Andrew stared back. "You're the only one in the fort who can speak the languages besides Joseph. And the natives respect you. I'm hesitant to send my men out at night. Joseph comes and goes freely, but he's already left to look for them. I wish he'd join the Cavalry."

"Joseph despises taking orders from anyone," Thad muttered, crossing to the base of the stairs. Where do we send our wives? We can't leave them alone *here*."

"No. It's out of the question."

"I suppose we could take them to Evaline's place. She wouldn't mind."

"Suz is armed. You realize you'll have to teach your wife to shoot."

Thad was halfway up the stairs by now. "Grab your pelisse, sweetheart," he said quietly. "We're taking you both to Evaline's."

Betsy looked up. "Why?"

"No questions, and be quick about it. I'll explain when we get back."

Betsy eyed him oddly, but did as he requested. A moment later they were standing in front of Evaline's back door. She answered with a rifle in her hands, but set it down when she realized who they were.

"We need to leave you with our wives," Andrew said quietly as she ushered them inside.

"Certainly. What's happening?"

"He swears he'll explain when he returns," Suzy answered with an irritated glance at her husband.

"Be vigilant, ladies, and bolt the doors," was the last thing Thad said as he disappeared out into the night.

* * *

Betsy was still staring at the door long after Evaline bolted it.

"Does this happen often?"

Suzy frowned. "More often than I'd like. I learned some time ago I'd have to learn not to sit here and imagine all the things that could happen to the men while they were outside at night. Most of the tribes value Andrew, and wouldn't hurt him. But there are a few rogues that are like Akecheta, who might."

Betsy felt sick to her stomach suddenly. She turned away, as Suzy put a hand on her shoulder.

"Betsy, I'll tell you one more thing. The natives like Thad, and they'd be loath to bring harm to him, or anyone with him. I feel better about Andrew just because Thad is with him. You'll get used to him being called on to do these types of things."

Betsy shook her head vehemently. Would she? The man she now called her husband was already dear to her. "Never," she said. "I'll *never* get used to it."

"Come, ladies," Evie suggested. "I just finished a

Queen's cake. Have a slice and take your mind off your worries."

Betsy followed Suzy into the small kitchen and sat down. The last thing she wanted was to eat, but she would force herself. Evaline set a slice of the delicious cake down in front of her, accompanied by fresh milk, saying, "Joseph brought milk and eggs by this evening right before he left. He keeps me supplied."

Suzy glanced up with a knowing expression. "Joseph the Longhunter?"

Evaline smiled. "He's good about bringing me things he gets in trade. I suppose he knows I need them."

But Betsy was still staring over her shoulder at the door, as if any moment she expected Thad to come back.

Chapter Six

aiting...

WIt was a long evening for all of them. Evaline watched as both ladies finally gave up on their vigil. Conversation had long ago ceased to exist, and she had placed one of the soft quilts across the wooden sofa. Suzy had fallen asleep on it. Betsy had paced until she was exhausted before she too sat down on the other end, leaned over on one arm and fell asleep.

Evie dragged her rocker up to the window, keeping her rifle at the ready. She'd warned Betsy away from the windows, and she was glad when the young bride had given up and fallen asleep.

This was a brutal country, much as she loved it. And these were brutal times. Perhaps she should have gone back east when her husband died. At least she could have slept at night without having her rifle by her side. Joseph often warned her to make sure she kept it handy.

Joseph the Longhunter.

He was a dear man, and she was more than a little fond of him. But after losing her husband in an attack two years ago, the thought of marrying again in this savage land was unthinkable.

Furious pounding from the back door brought her out of her reverie. She ran through the kitchen of the little shotgun house to the window, her rifle at her side, and looked out to see who it was. Thad and Andrew, and one more stood outside the door. She recognized him instantly. It was Joseph.

Quickly she unbolted the door and opened it.

"Come in, all of you."

"Sorry to put you out, Evaline," Thad said quietly.

"Did you find Mose and James?"

Andrew answered with a strained face, glancing at Suzy and Betsy to see if they were listening. When he found them sleeping, he nodded. "We did. Both dead. We buried them before coming back to the fort."

"Oh dear," Evie shook her head. "It was the new soldiers?"

"Yes. I feel as if I've failed their families."

Joseph shook his head at him. "Balderdash. Did you cause them to break out of the brig and run?"

"No, but—"

"Then we won't hear it. Not a word. Take your wife and go home and get some sleep." Joseph's voice was curt, and Andrew smiled.

"Will do, sarge."

Joseph grinned, his silvery beard glinting in the light of the oil lamp.

Evie turned to them. "Suzy fell asleep early. Betsy paced until I thought her feet would fall off before she finally gave up. Can I fix something to eat for you?"

Andrew made a face. "I haven't the least desire to eat after what we've seen this evening."

Thad agreed, but Joseph smiled at Evie. "*I* might. Still have some of those eggs I brought you?"

"I do. And I made a Queen's cake, although we ate part of it. But it won't take me a second to whip up some scrambled eggs and toast. Thad, what time should I come over this morning?"

"Whenever you wish. I intend to sleep in if I can."

"You men take your wives home," Joseph led the men through the house to the front room and waited, making sure Evaline was busy in the kitchen before he spoke.

"I'll stay until morning."

* * *

Thad approached Betsy and stared down at her a moment before lifting her into his arms. He felt as if he needed to bathe before joining her in their bed. The smell of death always made him feel this way. He wondered if he carried it on his clothes still. He'd helped to bury the bodies of both men so Andrew didn't have to do it alone.

A murmur from his bride let him know she didn't mind. Her arms were around his neck now.

"Thad..."

"It's me, sweetheart. Go back to sleep. I've got you, and I'm taking you home."

Her eyes opened suddenly, and he looked down to see they were on him. "What happened?"

"I'll tell you in the morning when you wake up."

Her scowl deepened. "You said you'd tell us when you got back."

"Tough. You aren't going to hear it right now. So go to sleep."

Her expression was unamused, but a moment later, she closed her eyes again and leaned her head against his shoulder.

"All right," she whispered. "Just this once."

"Good Lord," Andrew looked over at him with Susannah in his arms. "She's strong-willed, isn't she?"

"You have utterly no idea."

Waiting for Andrew to leave first, he followed, carrying Betsy outside.

"I'll get the door," Joseph said from behind him.

He carried her across the compound to his own house, keeping an eye out for signs of danger. None. The house was the same. He laid Betsy down on the sofa and checked the house for signs someone had been there.

Nothing. When he was satisfied, he made sure both doors were bolted, then carried her to the bedroom and undressed her. Then, he went to the back room to wash up before joining her.

In bed, Betsy turned to face him. His eyes were closed, his face drawn and weary as she studied him. His profile was no less handsome than it had been the first day she'd met him, but she knew he'd been through a horrific ordeal. She eased herself over him and wrapped her body around his, tucking her head up under his chin. When he wrapped her closely in his arms, she knew he was aware of her presence.

She gave a soft little sigh before falling asleep on top of him.

When she opened her eyes, the room was light, and Thad was gone.

"Thad?"

No sound. Betsy hurried to the wardrobe and chose a pale-yellow frock, dressing quickly.

She found Evie in the kitchen cooking when she approached.

"Thad has gone out for a minute. He said to tell you he'll be back shortly."

"He'd better be," Betsy grumbled under her breath. When she saw the surprised expression on Evie's face, she chuckled. "He promised he'd tell me what was going on last night and he still hasn't."

Evie's smile was knowing. "Sometimes, it's better not to know, Betsy. I've found that out, living in this wild land. Let me heat up your breakfast for you."

Later that morning...

Thad approached the house, wondering if Betsy was up. He'd left her curled up on her side early that morning, and kissed her soundly, but she hadn't awakened.

As he cleared the step to the back door, however, he had no doubt; he could hear her voice clearly from inside.

She didn't sound happy.

When he raised his fist to announce his presence, it opened. Evaline stood there, grinning.

"Thank you, Evaline." His eyes lit on Betsy's face as he entered and rested his hands on her shoulders.

"How's my girl this morning?"

"Waiting for you to tell me what happened last night."

His smile disappeared. "You're sure you really want to know."

"Yes."

"All right, then. Come with me. But I'll only answer the questions you ask me directly." He reached for her hand, tugging her up and out of her seat and leading her to the bedroom. Deciding to leave out as many details as he could, he began to tell her what had happened as he and Andrew had searched for the men the night before, and how they found them.

Before he finished, however, she had clapped her hand to her mouth as if she might vomit. He reached for a waste basket and brought it to her. Sitting down next to her, he held it in front of her just in time for her to lose her breakfast. His handkerchief, he brought to her mouth. "All right, Elizabeth," he said, "I hope you won't ask me again to explain what happens when I'm called to go on a hunt in the dark of night, because it isn't always pretty. Sometimes there are good endings. Not always."

"Did," she gasped for air, "the Indians do that?"

He frowned. "I can't tell you, because I don't honestly know. What we found wasn't typical of the work of *any* of the tribes here. I'm not exactly sure what to think, and I'm hesitant to suggest blame on *any* tribe for this. I'm thinking about it, sweetheart. Andrew agreed with me. I suppose it could have been done by warriors, but if so, they would have planted an obvious sign that pointed to themselves. There was nothing like that."

Betsy was staring through him now. "You don't think it was Akecheta?"

"I do not. Does that answer your question?"

"No. But you said there were problems between him and the Sioux chief. And if someone wanted to plant blame on another person—" she halted.

"Ah, you can see that even with your young eyes." He sighed. "There's a story behind him. Akecheta was once a favored warrior for the Sioux. He let his temper get the better of him once, and rumor is he beat one of Swift Eagle's daughters. He's been banned from the tribe. The woman is protected by the Sioux now, and he isn't allowed near the tribe any longer."

"Why did he beat her?"

He studied her face. "That's a question you'd have to ask her, and I hope you never have the chance to do it. It's their business and their story to tell, not ours." He squeezed her shoulders. "Feeling better now?"

"A little."

"Then I must leave you a bit. I need to pay Swift Eagle a visit and see if he's heard what happened to the soldiers we found last night. I promise to be back before long."

Betsy grabbed his hand. "Please, find out how Wapi is doing? And did you get to eat breakfast?"

He smiled and brushed her hair away from her face. "I will ask. And yes, I did eat. Thank you for thinking of me."

"I..." she licked her lips nervously, "*always* think of you."

Thad traced her lips slowly with his finger before lowering his head and planting a kiss on her mouth.

"That makes me happy, Betsy. Susannah will likely be over to visit this afternoon. And when I get back, I'll take you to visit Joseph at the Trading Post and see if you can choose some new goods for the curtains downstairs." He stood for a moment, watching her.

"And I'm very pleased that you want to give the material you have to Evaline."

He turned on his heel, and left, waving a goodbye to the housekeeper on the way past the kitchen.

"Shall I bolt the doors, sir?"

"Absolutely. It would be wise. For now." He said, closing the front door.

Waiting until he heard the bolt, he moved toward the captain's quarters. But as he glanced around, he could see that the inside of the fort was quite empty. The ladies he usually saw were apparently still at home, and even the soldiers he saw wore troubled expressions.

Bad news travels fast.

The thought occurred to him as he strode toward the Trading Post.

Joseph was inside now, looking refreshed, but the Trading Post was nearly empty.

"Morning, Thad."

"Morning. What do you have in the way of goods for windows?"

Joseph eyed him curiously. "Your new bride unhappy with your house?"

Thad grinned. "If she is, she isn't saying so. I offered to buy her some goods so she could put her own touch on the house." He glanced around the post. "Quiet this morning?"

Joseph leaned forward and spoke in a low voice. "Like a tomb. This hasn't happened in a long time. My advice? Keep your bride *inside*. I'll bring over some samples for her to see this evening. But Evaline said there were some goods in the crates that were nice. Figured the girl would use those."

Thad nodded. "She will be using them. Can you keep a secret?"

"I'm full of other people's secrets. Sure."

Thad lowered his voice. "Betsy plans on making Evaline some new curtains for *her* place. After I took her over there yesterday afternoon, she decided there would be enough to make some sofa cushions *and* make curtains. And you're not to spill it to anyone, either. *Especially* Evaline."

Joseph backed up. "Hmph. Guess I just thought about making sure she was well fed. Didn't think about the pretty stuff."

"I hear ladies *like* pretty stuff."

The door opened, and Thad looked up to see Andrew approaching. "I dropped off Susannah at your house, Thad. I'd like to go to Swift Eagle's with you."

Thad glanced at him thoughtfully. "That might be a good idea. I wanted to give him some assurance that we weren't jumping to conclusions about the murders last night." He turned to Joseph. "See you this afternoon, my friend."

The trader gave him a swift nod. "I'll escort Evaline home and then come back. She doesn't need to be walking alone across the fort."

* * *

The visit with Swift Eagle was less than satisfactory, but Thad felt the chief understood that they didn't blame the Sioux for the deaths of the soldiers.

Swift Eagle folded his arms across his chest. "What about warriors of Akecheta?"

Thad frowned. "I don't think he had anything to do with it either." Explaining his reasons, Swift Eagle gave a thoughtful nod. "Always trust you to be fair. Thank you."

"And," Thad added quietly, "my bride inquired if your son is feeling better."

There was a long silence. "Give our thanks," was all he said. As he followed them outside to their horses, he said, "Son getting worse. And," he added, "warriors unable to find Akecheta. Or his warriors. Camp empty."

"I see. Many thanks, Swift Eagle. Please let me know if I can help in any way."

Andrew gave him a nod as well, as they left.

Swift Eagle turned to his warriors. "Take them back in safety," he said in an authoritative voice. "Friends."

At the entrance to the fort, Thad turned to the warriors and waved to them, speaking to them in Sioux.

"What did that mean?" Andrew asked as they left.

"Always friends," he said solemnly.

Andrew's shoulders slumped. "Now comes the hard part. Now, it's time to gather the soldiers together and convince *them* of it."

"And that," Thad added, may not only be hard; it may be impossible."

Andrew nodded solemnly. "Indeed."

Thad and Andrew were pacing the floor downstairs, waiting on Joseph to arrive with Evie when a familiar pummeling sound reverberated through the house.

"It's Joseph," Thad said, glancing out the window. Joseph had his arms full of material goods. "He has Evie with him." Opening it, he motioned them inside. "Come in. Betsy and Suzy are upstairs with their heads together."

"Ah. Then Betsy will be wanting to see *this*. I brought goods for her to choose from for your curtains." Joseph frowned, glancing from one to the other. "You'll let me know how the meeting goes?" he asked. "I'll be here when you get back."

Thad nodded gratefully. "Thanks for staying with the ladies. We won't be gone any longer than we must." He shook his head as he crossed the fort to the hall.

Andrew frowned in his direction. "Suzy's a good shot, but not even my soldiers compare with Joseph. At least not around here."

The statement should have brought comfort, but it didn't. As they moved into the hall where the troops met, Thad found a group of angry men inside. Their heads were down, their voices muttering quietly. He didn't like what he heard.

Will Brent had taken a seat across from Thad, and seemed to be vigilant in watching the crowd. He *should*, Thad supposed. He was second in line. His eyes met Thad's as Andrew began speaking, and they exchanged a small nod.

Henry Lake was even in attendance; surprising, since he never attended any of these things. Thad wasn't sure who was watching whom more closely, but Henry seemed to be eyeing everyone with suspicion.

Thad found himself unable to relax, however, thinking of his bride at home. What must *she* be thinking about this? Did she realize the seriousness of it?

He hoped she did.

And he hoped she didn't.

He listened carefully as the meeting with the troops was called. Andrew carefully explained what he and Thad had found the night before, and told them about his suspicions. Convincing the men held difficulties, however. Half of the men had a desire to go to war instantly. Several more didn't know what to think, and some just looked as though they wanted to be anywhere but here. Thad knew it wasn't his place to share his opinion with them, and besides, Andrew was doing a good job. He had the respect of his men; that was obvious.

But as the meeting wore on, Thad began to have his doubts.

"I say, this means war." One of the soldiers spoke up.

Andrew moved toward him, staring him down. "Are you willing to be the first in line to lead it? And who will you war against? Because *I* won't lead it until I know for certain who committed the act."

The man stared at him.

"I won't lead a troop of men in a war against someone until I have proof that I know who's guilty. And I don't. I don't even have proof any of the tribes are guilty. Understand?"

There was more grumbling among the men. Across from him, Brent was glancing around at the group of soldiers. Thad wondered what he was thinking. He wore a frown on his brow Thad wasn't accustomed to seeing. Something else was amiss too.

What was it?

The growling continued as he listened. Andrew was trying to regain control of the crowd. However, Thad wasn't at all sure some of them wouldn't take matters into their own hands.

Not at all.

When the meeting was finished, Thad moved toward Andrew. Brent, however, was standing between them, and turned to him.

"That was close," he said,

Thad only nodded. "*Too* close."

Chapter Seven

A *t home that evening...*
Betsy was standing halfway down the stairs when Thad and Andrew left, and Evie crossed the room to her.

"Just pretend it's another day I'm here working, honey. I'll fix Joseph something to eat. You go upstairs and sew, and I'll send him up with the coffee when it's ready."

Betsy frowned. "Are you sure? I feel as if I'm a very poor hostess."

"I'm sure." She leaned forward, whispering. "Joseph and I get to spend very little time together. Go."

Betsy glanced at Joseph, who handed her the

armful of material, and smiled at him. "Thanks," she whispered.

"Just let me know when you decide which one you want, and I'll come up and get the rest."

With a nod, Betsy carried them up.

Suzy met her at the top and took them from her. "Oh my. How will you choose?" She set them down on the sewing table and began looking through the colors and patterns.

"I don't know. These are lovely, aren't they?"

"They are. I just made new curtains for the captain's quarters last fall, or I'd be begging Andrew for some of these." She glanced up. "Do they need refreshments downstairs?"

Betsy gave off a soft giggle. "No. Evie's making Joseph dinner, and she has officially dismissed me with orders to come up and sew."

"Ah. I see." Suzy's eyes were sparkling. "Those two are so amusing."

Betsy moved around the table, fingering the materials one by one. After two or three passes, she set her hand down on the one nearest Suzy. "What do you think?"

"That would be *my* choice." Suzy lowered her voice to a whisper. "But I love them all."

"And look at this," Betsy moved to the closet in the

upstairs bedroom and pulled out a large piece of material she'd managed to get from Joseph. "It's for Thad a winter jacket. But you aren't to tell him. His is getting worn."

Suzy clamped her lips tight as she shook her head. "He'll love it. And it'll keep him warm, all right. Of course, you know how men are. When a coat gets old, they think it's just getting *comfortable*."

"I didn't know that. But I won't get rid of the old one." She sat down in the rocker and heaved a sigh. I have another question. Have you seen this much unrest in the fort before?"

Suzy stared at her a long time before she answered. "No," she said softly. "It was bad last year before the treaty was signed. Then it got better. And Andrew tells me not to worry. He says it will improve as the days pass. I'm sorry. I wish I had a better answer."

Betsy nodded. "Do you think our men will be all right at the meeting?"

Suzy nodded. The men are loyal to Andrew, and to Thad. They might not like what he says but they'll listen. Except Henry Lake. But he really shouldn't be there. He once was a soldier here, but not any longer. Apparently, no one has told him he can't attend these things, though."

Betsy put her scissors down. "Since you're

speaking of Mr. Lake," she began, "I already don't like him."

Suzy's expression changed to one of sarcasm. "No one *likes* him. Him and his *healthy goats*. I keep waiting for them to get sick like everyone else's did. But they don't."

"What's Henry's weakness?"

Suzy turned to face her. "What do you mean?"

"Everyone has a weakness," Betsy returned. "Does he beat up on his wife, like Akecheta? Or—"

"He doesn't have a wife. Who in the world would live with that man?" Suzy sat down on the stool, edging it closer. "I suppose if he has one, it's drinking. And he often comes to the Canteen and plays poker. He has a foul temper when he loses, or so Andrew tells me."

"Does he win much?"

Suzy shrugged. "Almost always. But Andrew says when he loses, he always pays up."

Betsy was quiet a moment before she felt the mischievous smile that crossed her lips.

"*I* play poker."

Suzy's eyes widened. "No," she said. "*No*, don't even think it. Thad would be furious with you if you tried playing against Henry at poker. What even made that occur to you?"

Betsy's mouth twisted in thought. "I have my own reasons, and I don't know if I can trust you not to tell anyone."

"Oh, I wouldn't tell. Because you'd be in big trouble if Thad found out. Betsy, push it right out of your mind, my friend. You can't do it." Her shoulders slumped as she stared at her friend. "But you're not listening, are you?"

"Of course, I'm *listening*."

"But you're going to do just what you want, aren't you? I've only known you two days? Three? And already I recognize that look."

Betsy began folding the material and putting it away.

"I don't know *what* you mean," she said.

Thad left the meeting with an unsettled feeling in the pit of his stomach. The grumbling and growling among the men had been intense, and they hadn't listened to Andrew as much as he'd expected when it began.

"Whoa, my friend. Slow down," Andrew called, from behind him.

"Sorry. Just eager to check on Betsy."

"She'll be fine. Joseph is there, remember?"

"True enough. I still worry about her. Despite her big heart, she has a mischievous streak in her that's disturbing. She's planning something, and I haven't yet figured out what it is."

"Such as?"

Thad turned to glance at him. "I don't know. But I have my suspicions." He raised his fist to knock as they reached the front door. "And whatever she's planning is something I'm sure I won't approve of."

A few seconds later, he heard the bolt being lifted from the inside, and Joseph's head appeared.

"Come in. All's well here. How did the meeting go?"

"Not as well as we hoped. For a few moments I thought we were only a step away from war."

Joseph's mouth flattened. "Are you prepared for that? And are they?"

"None of us are," said Thad, shaking his head. "I need to pay a visit to each tribe tomorrow and let them know what's happened, and what *may* happen if the men don't calm down. And Andrew needs to speak with the men, one to one." He halted abruptly as he saw Betsy standing in the front room at the base of the stairs. Her eyes lit on his face and were wide and scared.

A wave of guilt passed over him suddenly for

taking her on as his wife. Would life have been better for her if she'd been able to continue with the wagon train? But just as quickly, it disappeared, remembering she wouldn't have been allowed to continue with the wagon train in any respects. And if he hadn't married her, she'd still be without protection.

Suzy was standing right behind her, three steps up, and her expression almost mirrored Betsy's. Andrew crossed the room to her instantly and took her into his arms.

"We'd better go, sweetheart. There may be men lined up at home to talk to me."

Suzy sent a glance toward Betsy. "I'll see you tomorrow. Remember what I said."

Joseph nodded, and reached for Evie's arm. "I'll take Evie home. Come by the post tomorrow and let me know what was said."

There was a nod from Thad. "Will do."

* * *

Betsy watched them go silently, feeling Thad's hands on her shoulders.

"Don't move, sweetheart. I'll be right back."

He moved quickly to the front door and bolted it, and returned, bringing the lantern with him. "Come with me." The order was soft but firm as he reached for her hand. "I should have showed you this before now."

Betsy let him lead her around the back of the staircase. Opening the door to the bedroom, he led her inside and closed it behind him. He took three steps to the right, moving aside the small rug on the floor and reached down.

"See this?"

She looked down as he held the lantern forward. There was a small slat, big enough for only one person and almost invisible, built into the floor. It was finished with the same pine as the floor and contained a small recessed knob. It too was nearly invisible. Thad lifted it and turned it a quarter of a turn. There was a click, as he gently applied pressure.

"Yes. I see it."

"Now, when you're trying to get back into the room you can twist it back the other way from underneath and turn it until it clicks again. Then the floor will open from the other side."

Betsy followed his directions as Thad took her hand and guided it down and backward, so the section of the floor was no longer visible.

She peered downward into the darkness. There was a ladder visible now and Thad began to lower himself down into the hole and climb down. Several feet down he reached for her.

"There's a hook built into the wall. When you get this far, hang the lantern on it and pull the rug back over the opening before you close the slat. See?"

"I see."

"Now, step backwards and climb down. I'll steady you."

Feeling nervous and uncertain, she began to climb down, until his hands were anchored around her waist.

"I have you now. Don't be afraid, pull the rug back into place and close the slat. And don't forget the lantern."

Gratefully, she followed his orders. Once she had the lantern in her hands, he lowered her to the earthen floor.

"That's all you have to do. I'll show you the tunnels. Stay beside me."

Betsy was glad he kept an arm around her. The tunnel was narrow and dark.

"How far down are we?" Her voice echoed as she spoke.

"About eight or ten feet. Count your steps from here. Out loud."

Betsy began to count, softly. Sixty steps later, they reached a wall, and Thad stopped her.

"Now, turn left and follow it until you see a door. For you, it may be more steps than mine. Perhaps ten or fifteen in all."

She found it, easily. When they were inside, she glanced around. There were some wooden cots, shelves lined with cans, and some chairs in a large area. A heavy bolt was fastened just inside the door. Betsy took the lantern over to examine the shelves.

"When was the food put here?"

"Recently. In the summer the twins have a garden behind their house, and raise fresh vegetables. They can it and bring some here. Other than that, the supply train brings it. It's not as good, of course, but it's nice to know it's here. And it's better than starving."

Betsy nodded. "When was the last time you had to stay down here?"

"I've never stayed here. This is for the ladies and wives of the soldiers who live in the fort."

"But not for you?"

Thad sighed. "Betsy, it's to keep you safe. If we get to that point, I'll be needed elsewhere to try to make peace." He gave her a grin. "And no, you can't stay above ground if that happens. The ladies down there will need you, for the same reason the above-ground folks will need me. And stop scowling." He pulled her to his side, grinning. "You're adorable when you scowl, you know that?"

Betsy ignored him, continuing to cast a morose expression his way. After a brief look around the room, he turned her back toward the tunnel outside, saying. "Let's go back. It'll be warmer at the house. I'm taking you back a different way. It's longer, but if you're upstairs, you may need the use of it."

She remained quiet as he guided her back through the tunnel in a different direction.

He was right; it was longer, and the rungs on the ladder more numerous. She realized they were going up to the second floor of the house when he stopped her. *This* time the trap door opened into the closet. Thad sent her up first on the ladder and came up close behind her.

"Don't worry. If you stumble, I'll catch you. Here, the hook for the lantern is on the other side. And the trap door opens *here*." He waited until she took hold of the recessed knob and slid the trap door to the side, then followed her up into the house. "If you're upstairs sewing, and you sense there's danger in the lower floor, you can still get to the tunnel. There is a lantern inside the closet and a box of long matches next to it, right here."

She nodded as he showed her where it was.

"Does everyone with two floors have two entrances to the tunnel?"

"Yes. But not everyone has an upper floor. Downstairs with you," he said into her ear as they reached the staircase. "And don't forget to blow out the lamp before you leave the tunnel and climb into the room. I'm taking you downstairs. Be ready for me to undress you, and then I plan on making love to you."

Betsy grinned at him as he gave her a gentle pat.

"And I hope," he said, smiling, "it's lovemaking you won't soon forget."

Betsy swallowed hard, as he turned her to face away from him and began easing her frock down off her shoulders. His touch was soft, yet determined as she felt it going lower and lower, first off one shoulder, then the other.

The chemise was next. Betsy found herself holding her breath as she waited.

Those hands; *those wonderful hands*. She found herself wondering how many times he'd done this, and stiffened under his hands. The memory of the morning before they married planted itself in her mind. He'd told her not to worry, he would teach her, and so far, he had been so good at doing just that.

Suddenly he turned her to face him. "And now," he said firmly, "what exactly did Suzy mean when she spoke to you before she left?"

Betsy averted her gaze. "What... do you mean?"

He turned her face back to meet his. "'*Remember what I said.*' Those were her exact words."

Betsy didn't answer. Instead, she attempted to turn away to avoid the intensity of his gaze. But Thad refused to let her, and turned her chin back to face him.

"Elizabeth? What do I need to do to get you to answer me? I distinctly remember letting you know on the day of our marriage there were to be no secrets between us."

Her eyes grew wide; she felt it.

"We only discussed the materials for Evie's house," she said, "upstairs in the sewing room."

He didn't believe her, she could tell. But he continued to stare down at her solemnly for several seconds before speaking. "I'll wait on you to come to me and tell me. But I will expect you to, sweetheart. Be mindful of that. If you don't tell me within a few days, I'll force the issue. And you won't like it."

Betsy met his eyes with penitence, and sighed.

How could she tell him what she had planned? There was an innocent little infant who needed sustenance not far away.

Thad reached over and lowered the wick on the lamp before he sat down on the side of the bed and lifted her up and over his lap. Raising her bottom high over his thigh, he slowly, softly, began to stroke her cheeks. Betsy gave a hiss as his hand stroked across her bottom. "And do you remember what I told you would happen if you lied to me?"

For an instant, she was tempted to tell him she would go to Chief Swift Eagle and tell him Thad had beat her. After all, he'd given sanction to a lady who had been beaten by Akecheta.

Then she remembered, however, the girl was the Chief's daughter, and groaned.

"Yes," Thad said softly, "you *do* remember."

Betsy closed her eyes. The sensuous feeling of his hand stroking across her bottom was decadent. "I'll tell you," she whispered, "very soon."

Thad had trouble removing his gaze from that little heart-shaped bottom. After all, it belonged to him, didn't it? He gave it a small pinch and listened to the squeal she emitted.

"You deserved that, young lady." When another sigh escaped her, he added, "Didn't you?"

"But you said," she glanced back at him over her shoulder, "you were going to make love to me."

"I did. And I will. But I want you to realize I'm paying attention. And you must know there will be consequences when you disobey me. Hear me?"

At her whimper, he lifted her into his arms, cradling her. Betsy glanced up into his face, frowning.

"I hear."

He planted a gentle kiss on her forehead; another on her lips followed before he turned to lay her down on the bed. Caging her to the bed with his arms, he brought his face down until they were nose to nose. "Already, Elizabeth, I care for you deeply. I won't have you doing things that hinder our relationship as man and wife. Nor will I have you planning things that might put you in danger. I hope you understand that."

"I do," she met his eyes in earnest now. "Oh Thad, I promise, I *do*."

His tongue invaded firmly, powerfully, as he kissed her, and she responded by receiving it eagerly. Each of them grew wilder as they began to love the other. Thad flipped her over on her belly and brought a pillow under her hips; Betsy began to grind her hips against his as he thrust into her, moaning with pleasure.

After allowing her to reach her peak several times, Thad insisted on reaching his own. Both of them came together at last.

They were lying together, when Betsy felt him stiffen over her.

"Thad?"

His hand covered her mouth suddenly, and he leaned down to her ear.

"Shh. The window."

Betsy turned to glance toward it. Outside was the shadow of a figure she could have sworn to be Akecheta. When she gasped, Thad's hand tightened over her mouth once more.

"Climb under the bed and stay there until I come back."

"I will." Betsy whispered in the smallest of voices as he dragged her from the bed and wrapped her in the quilt, before shoving her under it.

Silently she watched him in the darkness as he once again dragged on his shirt and trousers, followed by his boots and his gun belt. Picking up his weapon, he tucked it into his holster. With a motion for her to stay, he left the room.

The last thing she heard was the click of the key in the lock.

* * *

Betsy wasn't sure when her eyes drifted closed, but a voice called to her. She'd fallen asleep?

"Sweetheart, you can come out now."

Thad's voice.

Betsy opened her eyes to see him leaning down and reaching for her. The room was slightly lighter inside now. It must be first light. She took the hand he offered, and let him guide her out from under the high bed.

"Thad?"

"Shh." He put a finger to his lips, motioning her to be silent.

As she rose up on tiptoe, she brought her mouth to his ear. "What happened?"

"I'll tell you later—" But she was already tapping her foot on the wooden floor and appearing impatient, and he shook his head. "I promise. Behave yourself." Helping her into bed, he tugged her close within his embrace. and prepared to whisper quietly into her ear.

She interrupted before he had a chance to speak, however.

"The shadow looked like Akecheta."

"It was. He needed to talk. I had to get him out of the fort before first light."

"But—"

"Don't talk. Just listen. I can't share with you what he told me, but if what he said is true, *he* knows, and now *I* do. And everyone in Fort Laramie is in danger. Dear God, I can't imagine why I brought you into a life with me at this time."

She turned in his arms to face him. "We didn't have a choice, Thad. *Either* of us. Jack wasn't about to let me go on with the wagon."

"I know. I *know*. But it doesn't help any to think I've put you in this kind of danger."

"But you *didn't*."

"Listen to me, sweetheart. If I allow anything to happen to you, I've failed you, and I've failed myself. Then there's the whole fort to think about."

"But they aren't just your responsibility. They're everyone's, aren't they?"

He took her face in his hands, staring down at her. "If I'm the only one who knows who's responsible, it's mine. *Only* mine."

He turned her back to face away from him, and held her against his chest.

"It's not fair," she whispered into the darkness. "Not at all."

"Did anyone ever tell you, sweetheart," he asked softly, "life isn't fair?" At her sigh, he added, "Be still now, and sleep. I need to think."

Chapter Eight

C *alming...*

Betsy half expected Thad to send her through the tunnel the next day.

He didn't.

He seemed to have a plan, and was extremely thoughtful. At night, they made love. It seemed to grow more passionate each night, and she suspected it helped him relax. She couldn't be sure, however. There were times when he was even tense during their episodes of lovemaking. He was quiet at meals, and held her in his lap for long periods of time. Andrew and Susannah were over frequently in the evenings, and Suzy was there many times in the afternoons to spend time with Betsy.

She watched her husband carefully. There was something going on here.

And whatever it was... was terribly, *terribly wrong*.

The cape...

It was several days before Betsy had the chance to get out of the house alone. She'd spent her time at the treadle, working on the things for Evie's house, and finished them.

The following Tuesday, however, Evie took the day off, and Thad was gone. He hadn't told her where he was headed, but his face held worry; she recognized that look well. Following him to the door, she waited until he kissed her goodbye and bolted the door behind him.

Standing quietly on the other side, she waited until he walked away. A moment later, however, she spotted him cantering toward the gates on Wellsy, his horse.

She scowled. Was he going to talk to Swift Eagle? Every day she'd wondered about the baby, and how he was doing, but when she asked Thad about him, his answers were evasive. That must mean the infant wasn't doing well. Surely if he was better, Thad would tell her. That would be good news, at least.

There were soldiers in the fort, and rather than let them see her, she moved through the house and opened the back door. The prairie winds were ferocious outside, and as soon as she opened it, she closed it again and went in search of her pelisse. She was glad she'd braided her hair today. Thad hadn't seemed to notice. He liked it when she wore it down, but the outside winds would make it a mess if she did. Finding the dark blue garment, she wrapped it around her and pulled the hood over her head. Taking a deep breath, she took a glance around outside before opening the door again.

The sharp winds blew in her face, and she closed her eyes against them as she shut the door and carefully made her way toward the Trading Post. A week or so earlier Thad had taken her to see Joseph and bought her some linen material and some new bright colored threads. She'd embroidered them with prairie flowers and crocheted the edges of them with matching threads. They were now cleaned, pressed and carefully wrapped in brown paper tied with ribbon; She checked to make sure they were still inside her pocket and ready to take to the post to see if Joseph might want them to sell.

She thought of the different kinds of fur sold at the post; mink, buffalo, beaver. However, fur wasn't the only thing available there. There were few ladies in the fort, but enough so there might be a place to sell them. She'd already given one to Suzy and Evie, and one each to Permelia and Cordelia, who seemed delighted with them. She half expected Joseph to shake his head and say they were frivolous, but she wouldn't know until she asked, would she?

Stepping inside the post, she heaved a sigh of relief, away from the winds. The wood stove in the corner had made the place nice and cozy. It wasn't as crowded as it usually was, though.

She looked around for Joseph. At first, she didn't see him. She did, however, get a good look at some of the things there, and moved toward the stove, rubbing her hands together for warmth. The shelves were full of material goods, and she eyed it as she warmed herself.

Suddenly, she saw it; a velvet cape hanging in the window, it's color a delicate ruby red. Glancing down at the worn pelisse she wore, she wondered what the price was.

"Oh my," she whispered, approaching it and

fingering the material gently. She wondered if Joseph could possibly get the material to make one. If so, how much would it cost her?

"Like it?"

She jumped in surprise, turning to see a tall gentleman behind her. It was Will Brent. He was smiling, but his mouth was half-twisted into a smirk today, different than the day he'd come to visit after the wedding.

"Very much," she glanced around the room, "but it's likely more than *I* could ever afford."

"With a lovely lady like you, perhaps we could work something out?" The smirk increased.

The words stung. How dare he? She turned to face him, her shoulders back. Standing as straight and tall as she could, she made her voice sharp.

"Exactly *what* do you mean by that remark?"

As if her response surprised him, he put both hands out in front of him. "Now, *now*, don't take offense. I was just trying to be polite."

"Be polite somewhere else." Another voice spoke from behind him. Joseph appeared, and stood between Will and Betsy. "Or perhaps I'll have to tell Thad you're being a little too familiar with his bride."

Will shook his head, and backed away, and Joseph turned to face Betsy.

"What can I help you with, Elizabeth?"

Forgetting the cape, and Will, she pulled one of the wrapped brown packages from her pocket and held it out toward him. "Actually, I was looking for *you*. I made these, and I wondered if perhaps I could sell them here. Or barter for some goods, or..." She watched quietly as he sent one last glance toward Will. Then he nodded.

"Come with me."

She followed him over toward the counter and watched as he carefully tugged at the ribbon on the first package, then the second.

A whistle escaped. "You said *you* made these?"

"Yes."

"What else do you make?"

Betsy gave a thoughtful pause. "Hair adornments, garments, ladies' undergarments, slippers..." She halted abruptly. "Joseph?"

But Joseph had already slipped into another realm. His gaze seemed to be somewhere else. Finally, he turned to her. "I see opportunities here, Elizabeth. Ladies in the fort are always asking me for things I've no way of getting. I have a proposition for you. Suppose you make one each of those things and let's see what they'll bring?"

Excitement crept into her voice. "Really?"

"Yes. And these?" He held up the handkerchiefs. "With your permission, I'll put them out on display. That should tell us how quickly they sell, and I'll look through my catalogue and see if there's anything to compare them to. That way I might know what we can get for them." He pulled out a catalogue and began turning the pages before shoving it toward her. "This is the nearest thing I see. If I provide the materials, and give you seventy percent of the final price, would it be worth your time to make them?"

Betsy leaned down to glance at the price. Seventy percent? That was a lot more than she'd expected. Eagerly, she held out a hand. "It's a deal, sir," she said, adding, "only, don't tell Thad I was here?"

Joseph frowned. "You're asking me to lie?"

She bit her lip. "No, not... *lie* exactly. Just don't volunteer any information."

Joseph threw back his head and laughed. "You're a swift one. All right."

She drew closer. "I have another question for you. I was wondering..."

His brows rose. "Yes?"

She glanced around to make sure there was no one else nearby, and lowered her voice. "If you could possibly arrange a game of poker with Henry Lake."

The color left his face. "You're out of your mind,

missy. No one in this territory has won a game with him for the last five years. *I* can't afford to play with him."

"Oh," she shook her head. "I'm not asking *you* to play with him."

He cocked his head to one side. "Thad sure won't."

Betsy sighed, and frowned. "I thought not. But if you could get enough men together for a game, I suppose that only leaves one person to join in, then."

Joseph stared at her. "Who?"

Betsy frowned at his expression.

"*Me.*"

She watched as the remaining color evaporated from his face. She reached out to steady him quickly.

"Joseph? Are you alright?"

"You—*you're* not considering playing poker with him!"

"My father taught me. He was a ruthless player. I'll never forget the look on his face the first time I beat him. I'm quite sure I'd be alright. Please Joseph, it's important I do this." She held a hand out in a plea, but he stared at it. blinking, before returning his gaze to hers.

"Oh, Miss Betsy. You've no idea what you're asking

of me. Thad will kill me, for sure. Dead, I'm telling you."

"He won't."

"You don't think so, eh?"

"No, I don't," she said, turning back toward the door. Then she stopped, facing him.

"He'll kill *me*."

* * *

Betsy had barely gotten out of the Trading Post when she spotted Suzy leaving the captain's quarters and headed toward her house. Knowing she had to get home before Suzy got there to avoid her friend's curious questions on where she'd been, she quickly ducked into an ally between two of the buildings.

She halted, suddenly. Lt. Brent stood directly in front of her.

"I *heard*," he said.

Oh dear God. He'd heard *all* of it?

"Hello." Her voice was uneasy, and he held up a hand.

"Don't be afraid. I have no ill intentions toward you."

She eyed him suspiciously. "No?"

"No. I know when I've been rebuffed. And I

promise not to tell Thad where I saw you today. But I am curious, and I have two questions."

She looked at him thoughtfully. "About what?"

"First, I saw the handkerchiefs Joseph is putting out for display."

"Yes?"

"You sew very well. I have a uniform shirt that has a small tear. If I bring it to you, could you mend it for me? I'll be happy to pay you."

"I can do that," she answered uncertainly. "And the second?"

"I want to know why you want to arrange a poker game with Henry Lake. He's a dishonest soul if ever I knew one. He cheats, and no one is able to win against him."

She averted her gaze. "I'm not sure I want to tell you."

He eyed her for a second. "Fair enough. You don't have to, of course. I was just curious. And I thought I *might* be able to arrange a game for you." He continued to watch her for a second, adding, "And I also might be able to arrange a few players to join the game. We'd be there to protect you, of course." He shrugged, and turned to leave.

Betsy bit her lip. Could she trust him? Not on her life. But did she have any other choice?

"Wait!" Her voice had an insistent ring to it when she called out.

He stopped and turned to face her.

"I..." she paused. "Henry has healthy goats, and there's a baby who needs goat's milk. That's all."

There was silence between them for a moment. "I know everyone here," he said. "And I'm not aware of anyone in the fort who has a new baby. Unless it's *outside* the fort?"

Another silence.

Betsy stared at him. She'd already said too much. But it was too late now.

"Does it matter? An infant who needs help is worth saving, no matter who they are."

His expression softened. "I suppose you're right. I'll see what I can do." With a nod, he turned, saying over his shoulder, "Be ready for a game on Saturday. That's when he usually visits the canteen."

Saturday. This is Thursday.

Betsy bit her lip. Could she really do this?

She waited until he was gone and peeked back out from between the buildings. Suzy was nearly at her front door now. Racing around the back, she reached the back door and opened it, bolting it behind her and running through the house. Breathing hard, she unbolted the front door and stood there, staring at Suzy.

"I thought you weren't home," Suzy remarked. "And you're wearing your pelisse. Have you been gone?"

Betsy felt her face grow hot. "Please don't tell Thad. I took some things I made to Joseph to see if he could sell them for me. Handkerchiefs I embroidered and crocheted, like the one I made for you." Her speech was rapid and she knew it was full of guilt. "He said he'd give me seventy percent of what he got for them. *If* they sell, that is."

"Whoa. They'll sell. There's no doubt."

"Evie didn't come today but she left us a cake from yesterday. Want a slice?"

"I'd love one. It'll take my mind off what's happening in the fort."

Betsy turned to the pie safe and took out the cake, cutting it and placing it carefully on the plate. Turning back to Suzy, she set it down, and said softly with a grin. "It's a bribe, actually. "Sweets for information. What *is* happening?"

"Ah. I love these kinds of bribes. But save it. If I knew, I'd tell you, bribe or no bribe. Andrew isn't telling me anything, except that if war breaks out, I should go to the shelter. There's a tunnel that leads underground. If we have war, you should come, too. And if so, we're to stay there until either he or Thad come to get us."

Betsy stopped with her fork halfway to her mouth. "No one else is to come for us?"

Suzy shook her head. "No one else. Not even Joseph."

Betsy stared at her. "That's odd. Don't you think so?"

Suzy chewed a bite thoughtfully.

"Yes," she said, finally. "I definitely do."

It was late in the afternoon when Thad came home. Both girls had been seated in the upstairs sewing room deep in conversation when he pounded on the door; he could hear footsteps hurrying down the steps shortly before Betsy glanced out the window, smiling at him.

A second later, the bolt was lifted and he was inside.

"Is Susannah here?"

"Yes, she's upstairs. Why?"

"Andrew's right behind me." He waited until Andrew was inside before taking the bolt from Betsy's hands and replacing it. "Have we enough to feed extra guests for supper, sweetheart?"

"Certainly. I'll fix it. Evie didn't come today."

"I know." He bent to place a kiss on her forehead. "You'll be fine."

Betsy turned toward the kitchen to see that Suzy was already there, setting out plates and flatware. When she looked up, grinning, Betsy mouthed a silent *thank you* to her.

"That's what friends are for," Suzy said back, under her breath.

An hour later, a supper of beans and cornbread were on the table and hot. Butter was smeared liberally over the cornbread and the ham and beans Evie had left them the day before were ready.

They ate quietly, however. Betsy eyed Thad and Andrew, noting that there seemed to be a coolness between them. Had she missed something previously? Suzy noticed it too; she kept glancing back and forth between them, and occasionally at Betsy. As soon as supper was finished, Andrew gathered his wife to his side.

"Time to go home, Suz," he said quietly.

"But—I was going to help with the dishes."

"I'll get them, Suzy." Betsy's voice was quick. "It'll be no trouble at all."

Suzy scowled. "All right, but I'll owe you." They had almost made it to the door when she left Andrew's side and moved to whisper in Betsy's ear. "I'll see you tomorrow. See if you can get Thad to talk. I'll try to do the same with Andrew."

Chapter Nine

T*roubles...*

Betsy merely nodded at Suzy's words as she watched the couple leave. What was going on between the two men? She hadn't seen either of them react this way before, and it wasn't like Thad to be rude to his best friend. Frowning, she turned to go into the kitchen and clean up, but her husband stopped her.

"Let the dishes sit a second, sweetheart." Drawing her to the sofa, he lifted her into his lap.

She tilted her head. "It's unlike you both to act this way," she said. There was censorship in her voice; she knew it.

His gaze lit on her, studying her for a second. "We had a minor argument. I was hoping he'd open up during supper, but he didn't."

"*Minor* arguments should be resolved before it's too late. That's what Papa always said. He didn't like it when Mama and I argued.

His mouth lifted on one side. "What about when *he* and your mother argued?"

Betsy chewed her lip thoughtfully. "I only heard them argue once."

He straightened. "Are you serious?"

She nodded. "And Mama was right. Papa told me that later."

"So," he cocked his head, "all the rest of the time she was wrong?"

"No. All the rest of the time she agreed with him. If she'd thought he was wrong, she'd have said so." She grinned at him. "They agreed on almost everything. At least that's what she told me once." She leaned back and tilted her head toward him. "What about you and Andrew? Do you agree with him all the time?"

Thad took her hands in his. "Andrew and I," he said quietly, "Are both of strong opinions. We do agree much of the time, which is much better than the troop captain before him. But when we *disagree*, it's hard to convince either of us the other is right. Sometimes it's necessary to part and think things through for a day or two."

"Ah. So, you're both strong-willed."

He lifted a brow. "Is that what you think?"

When she nodded, a grin widened across his mouth. He hugged her to him and set her on her feet. "Let's go clean up the kitchen, sweetheart. Then, I'm taking you to bed and ravishing you."

"I look forward to it." She grinned, and began tugging him toward the kitchen.

"Ah. I see the twinkle in those impish eyes. I can't wait."

But when she began adding extra steps to the cleaning of the kitchen, he leaned against the counter and gave her a glare.

"You're stalling, young lady."

Betsy gave a giggle. "It took you long enough to notice."

Suddenly she found herself thrown over his shoulder and a sharp slap planted on her bottom.

"Stop it!" She began to protest. "What was that for?"

"Let that be a lesson to you," he said, taking her toward the bedroom. "Don't provoke your husband."

Above her, Thad stared down into her face as she looked up. There were furrows across her brow. Something was obviously worrying her. He stopped, smoothing his hand across her soft skin.

"What is it, my love?"

She met his gaze. "What is *what*?"

"This," he said, smoothing his hands over them once again. "Something has you worried."

She shrugged. "It's nothing. Really. Just everything that's going on with the fort. And I worry about you."

He eyed her, suspicion making its way down his spine. "Are you sure that's all?"

There was a long pause. "I'm sure," she said in a whisper.

A feeling in the pit of his stomach caused his wariness to show. "Betsy—"

But as he spoke, she reached up, tracing a gentle finger down his jaw and lifted her face off the pillow to kiss him. A moment later, her tongue entered, inviting him inside.

Lowering his head to hers, he entered her mouth swiftly, powerfully. Forcing her head back down on the pillow, he took possession of her and entered her with a swift thrust.

* * *

Betsy lay there for a long time, staring into the darkness, tucked up against his chest. She felt like she'd committed a horrible crime by distracting him with lovemaking when he'd asked her a question. How could she have done this? If Thad found out what she was planning, he'd never, ever again trust her. She'd have to keep him occupied tomorrow throughout the day. Wondering how she'd manage to get away from the house on Saturday, she tried to make plans.

It was late when she managed to fall asleep, dreaming of poker games and an evil man, whose face she had not yet seen.

* * *

Found out...

If Betsy thought Henry Lake's face was evil in her dreams, she was unprepared to see it in real life. He was a tall man with a craggy face, thick black eyebrows and even blacker eyes. When Joseph brought her into the canteen, Will Brent was the first to glance up. There was a pile of cash in the middle of the table, and quite a few coins. It was obvious Henry had partaken heavily of the whiskey. He stared at her a long time, looking her up and down, and nodded to Will.

"This the one?"

Will acted much as if he didn't know her, but nodded back. "Yep."

"Supposin' I win against this little filly? What's my prize?"

Betsy sat down in the empty chair, staring back at him and forcing a smile. "Money, sir. That's all. And supposing *I* win? What's *my* prize?"

Henry scowled back at her a second before a smile crossed his face. "You, little lady, can have whatever you want."

"Right, then." Betsy forced her voice to become serious. "Shall we begin, gentlemen?"

An offer of whiskey from her right caused her to look up. "I never drink while I play at cards," she said with a smile. "But you can leave it there until I'm finished. *Or*," she added, "you can give it to Mr. Lake."

Henry reached for it before she began dealing, and took a gulp.

Will handed her a new deck of cards, and she began shuffling. Her movements were deft, and a few seconds later every man at the table was staring at her. She glanced from one to the other with a smile, and continued.

"Game?"

A wicked grin crossed Henry's face. "Five card draw."

"As you wish."

Betsy watched the faces of the men just as they watched her.

Aware that people were coming and going from the canteen, she tried to concentrate on the game. Taking a deep breath, she began.

Suzy knocked on the door once, twice, three times. Leaning forward, she peeked in through the window only to find it dark. She stood there, frowning.

Where was Betsy?

"Suz? What are you doing?" Andrew's voice called to her, and she turned. He and Thad were riding toward the house. A moment later both had dismounted and were standing next to her.

"I had planned to check on Betsy's progress with the curtains..." Suzy's voice faded as she looked from one to the other.

"When Andrew and I left, she was upstairs sewing," Thad answered calmly. He tried the door, but it was bolted from the inside. He began pounding on it thunderously.

Andrew glanced behind them. "I noticed the canteen was full. There must be a game going on."

He had barely spoken when Suzy gave a huge gasp. "Oh, dear God! No, *no*! She *didn't*!"

Thad turned to her, his voice hard.

"She didn't *what*?"

Suzy gulped and met his gaze as if she didn't know what to say. Andrew stepped forward and took her chin in his hand.

"Susannah. Answer him."

Instead of speaking, her eyes flew toward the canteen.

"Oh, God." Thad barely spoke before he took off running.

It was dreadfully stuffy inside the canteen, with all the people crowded around. For a moment, Betsy considered having a drink of the whiskey from the glass before her. Then she noticed Henry Lake was about to put his hand under the table, and she sat up straight. So, this was how Henry won; he *cheated*.

"Hands within sight, please, gentlemen." Her address was to the whole table, yet her gaze was straight at Henry.

Both his hands were visible now, she could see that, and nodded. "Thank you."

The other players had dropped out, placing their cards before them. Will and Henry were left playing, along with her. Betsy did a quick mental calculation.

This could be bad.

She looked down at her cards again.

A moment later, Brent laid his cards down. "I'm out."

An evil smirk crossed Henry's face. "Well, now. Isn't that a sight?" He put his cards down. "A full house. And you, little lady?"

Betsy stared at him a few seconds, before a smile began its way across her face.

Slowly, she made a show of setting her cards down so they faced him. An Ace, King, Queen, Jack and a ten, all of the same suit stared upward.

Henry's face was apoplectic. Betsy worried for a moment he would explode, as whistles and cheers filled the air around her. Apoplexy turned to disbelief before his shoulders slumped. With a resigned sigh, Henry stood to his feet, reaching into his pockets.

She shook her head. "Oh, but Mr. Lake, I don't want your money."

His expression changed to one of incredulousness as she leaned forward, putting her chin on her hand. "You said I could have whatever I wanted." A moment later, she spoke again.

"And what I want," she said, "is a healthy mama *goat*."

* * *

Henry seemed to forget where he was standing, and that there was a table between them. He started toward her just as she heard the sound; the hammer of a pistol being cocked from over her head. A hand pressed down on her shoulder, keeping her in place as she heard an angry voice speaking from behind her.

"You heard my wife, Henry. A goat it will be, and one of her choosing."

Henry's jaw was pulsing. After a long moment, he looked from one to the other and gave a silent nod.

"Come with me."

The glare Betsy received from Thad when she looked up at him sent a tingle down her spine. He took her hand in his with a firm grasp and leaned forward, speaking in a low growl.

"You are in *so* much trouble, young lady,"

"But," she whispered back, "can it wait until we deliver the goat?"

"Oh yes," he replied. "It'll take me at least that long to calm down."

With a tug, he led her out to follow Henry. Will, Andrew, Joseph and several others followed, too.

"We'll go along," said Andrew, "To make sure she gets what she bargained for." Andrew's glance at Thad on the way out was one she wondered if Suzy had ever seen..

* * *

"Oh, she'll get what she's bargained for," Thad muttered to himself on the way out the door, ignoring Betsy's wide eyes as she glanced up at him. He lifted her up onto Wellsy's back, and the others followed on their horses. Along the way, the Sioux warriors joined the parade.

Keeping up with Henry wasn't difficult. He did well to stay on his horse at all, after all the whiskey he'd consumed. Thad wondered if Henry would even remember the transaction the following day.

And half hoped he *wouldn't*.

The inhabitants of the fort were curious; they, too followed the parade of soldiers who kept up with Henry's lead. Andrew provided a cart from the fort for the livestock, and it rattled along behind them. Thad didn't look at them. He kept his eyes straight ahead and kept Betsy pulled back against him until they reached Henry's land.

Thad had always marveled at the land Henry owned. It was vast, and how he'd managed to keep his animals from contracting the dreaded anthrax plague, no one knew.

But he had.

Henry turned back to nod toward them as he stopped the horse at his gates.

"Keep your horses outside the gates," he ordered. "I don't want my livestock exposed to any diseases they might carry."

No one bothered to argue with him. They dismounted outside and followed him in on foot as he made his way toward the pasture.

The goats were separate from the other livestock when they reached the pasture. Thad kept Betsy close to his side with his arm tightly fastened about her waist. When she reached the goats, she leaned up on tiptoe, close to his ear.

"Please help me choose, Thad. After all this, I don't want to make a mistake."

His simple nod answered her.

He *did* help her choose; a mother goat with a baby next to her.

"Might as well take the kid too," Henry growled.

"It'll die without her." He stared at Betsy for a long moment before breaking out into laughter. "Got to hand it to you, missy. You won, fair and square. Never saw a woman play like that."

Thad watched as his wife returned Henry's smile.

"Thank you, sir," she said softly. "You were quite good *yourself*."

Henry's grin disappeared. "But don't ever ask me to play against you again. Thad, keep your eye on your bride."

Thad gave him a distinct nod. "I fully intend to."

The warriors of Swift Eagle were waiting outside Henry's gate when Thad and Betsy reached them with the mama and baby in tow. Henry lifted the goat and the kid into the cart with more gentleness than was expected, and turned away to lock the gates behind him.

He did not look back.

Thad turned to the warriors that had followed. "Please, take us to Swift Eagle?" he asked. "My wife has gifts for his son."

The warriors nodded; solemness filled their faces until they turned away toward the fort. But in the next moments, he could see one or two of them glancing back at Betsy. Their expressions had changed into smiles now. She had certainly won their admiration; that much was clear.

He too, found it hard to keep a smile from his own face. *Poker*? How had she arranged it without his knowing? Yes, he'd have a word or two to share with Joseph and Will and the others; even more to share with Betsy. She was never to try this again. Ever.

But his chest swelled as he glanced down at the top of her reddish-blonde curls. They bounced in the breeze as Wellsy kept pace with the warriors.

Try as he might, he couldn't help being extremely proud of his bride.

Betsy thought the journey to the Sioux village would never end. Swift-eagle was waiting outside his tent as they approached. He eyed the goats in the cart as Thad set Betsy on her feet and turned to unload them. His stern face moved from one to the other as Thad brought the animals to him.

"What is this?"

"A gift," Thad said softly, "from my wife."

"For your son," she added. "Goat's milk."

Swift Eagle blinked twice as she observed him.

Betsy thought for a moment he was going to cry. Then, he turned toward the tent.

"Come, quickly. Son *very* sick."

They followed him inside to witness a solemn scene. Wachiwi sat inside the teepee on the far side holding her son and weeping. Next to her was another young woman with her hands clasped together and tears streaming down her face. There was a man close by, with a long robe and some symbols on the back Betsy didn't understand. He was chanting in their language, and drawing images on an animal skin. Between his incantations, he would pick up a small gourd and shake it, making noises. Over a fire, he stirred a foul-smelling mixture in a metal pot.

Swift Eagle nodded to the medicine man as he turned. The expression on his face indicated his desire to know if he should stop, but the chief motioned to him to continue. However, he brought the mother goat into the tent along with the baby and indicated to Wachiwi that she could begin the milking process.

Wachiwi's tears increased, however, Betsy was almost convinced they had turned to tears of joy. She steeled her face to keep it solemn as she glanced up at Thad. He had done the same. Her father would have called this a 'poker face', had he lived.

With a small amount of milk now in a metal bowl,

Wachiwi began dipping her fingers into it and letting the milk drip down into the infant's mouth.

The scene was amazing as Betsy watched. The infant sucked the milk from his mother's fingers almost eagerly, as if nothing had ever tasted so good. Silence fell over the teepee as they all sat, mesmerized.

All except one. The medicine man stared at the potion he had mixed over the fire, glancing up at the chief. He spoke in a low voice to Swift Eagle, who gave a slight shake of his head and raised a hand to stay his motion.

Betsy wondered what the medicine man meant to do. Had he planned to give the mixture to the infant? She dared not ask; instead, she only stood there, keeping her eyes on the chief's son. Wachiwi seemed relieved, and so did the younger woman nearby.

A moment later, the medicine man snuffed out the fire and rose. Picking up the mixture, he set it aside. The animal skin he'd drawn figures on, he snatched, folding it under his arms, and with one last look at Betsy and Thad, he left the tent.

Swift Eagle held up a hand to them, motioning them to stay where they were, and followed. Loud voices were heard outside, and Betsy looked up into her husband's face, her eyes wide. A slight shake of his head was the only answer he gave.

The infant opened his eyes again, and his mother dripped more of the precious milk into his mouth. He slurped it with enthusiasm, and Wachiwi waited until he was asleep before handing the infant over to the younger woman.

"Mika," she said softly as if to introduce them, then motioned to Betsy. "Bet-see."

The young woman looked more like a girl than a woman when she smiled. Betsy gave her a brave smile back, and Wachiwi moved closer to her. Throwing her arms around Betsy's neck, she held on tightly, as if she'd never let go.

Betsy was touched, and Wachiwi's shoulders began to shake with silent sobs as the two of them held on to each other.

They moved apart as Swift Eagle re-entered the teepee. An expression of concern lit his face as he turned to Thad.

"Paytah not understand. Son not need potion. Need milk." He turned to Betsy and smiled. "We thank you. You bring most precious gift."

Thad nodded. "From Betsy. We must go. Thank you for accepting it."

"Warriors guide you back." He paused a few seconds, cocking his head. "How?"

Betsy, confused, glanced back at him. "Pardon?"

"How you get goat? And baby?"

Thad glanced at her before answering. "She arranged a poker game with Henry Lake, and won. What she asked for was one of his female goats."

Swift Eagle's stare at Betsy filled with disbelief.

"You..." His voice disappeared before he took a breath. Suddenly he began to bellow with laughter. Putting both hands to his belly, he couldn't stop, and finally waved them away.

Betsy could hear him as Thad led her outside the tent, speaking in Sioux to Wachiwi and Mika, but he still couldn't stop laughing.

When Thad leaned down to her ear, he didn't sound quite as amused.

"You have a big heart, young lady," he growled softly. "But I hope you're prepared for the consequences of your actions today."

Chapter Ten

C

onsequences...

Paytah, the medicine man was standing outside the teepee when Thad lifted Betsy up onto Wellsy's back and then mounted the horse himself. The look on Paytah's face was full of hatred.

"Thad," Betsy said softly, "look."

"I see. Keep your eyes straight ahead, sweetheart. The warriors will surround us."

They did. Betsy, however, could feel the eyes of the medicine man on her as they left the teepee of Swift Eagle, and shivered. Her husband tightened his arms around her, however, comforting her. When the warriors left them at the gates of the fort, Betsy felt rather than heard, her husband's deep sigh of relief.

They were home.

The spanking Betsy received that afternoon over her husband's knee was not something she wanted to repeat. *Ever.* It ended, however, with her begging his forgiveness and promising never to go behind his back and do anything like it again. He held her long afterward, cuddling her closely and telling her how much he cared for her. But when she asked if she could go and visit baby Wapi again, his answer was firm.

"Not unless I go with you. Paytah may take a while to calm down, and I won't have you fearing his retribution."

"But—but the baby should thrive on the goat's milk. Why would that upset him?"

"I'm not certain just how to explain it, sweetheart. He's proud, and to him it appears you've usurped his position. He was prepared to give what we might think of as Last Rites."

"Will you go and see them, then, and bring me reports on him?"

Thad was silent a moment. "You're quite a determined little one, aren't you?"

"Well," she answered slowly, "I just want to know how he's doing. I want so much for him to be well again, as a baby should be."

Thad bent to kiss her forehead. "Such a big-hearted girl you are. Yes. I'll bring reports on his welfare, as long as you promise to obey me and do as I tell you. I can't have you in danger, my love. And tell me. Did Joseph know you were planning this shenanigan today?"

She averted her gaze. "I... think you should ask *him*."

"I'm asking *you*, Elizabeth."

A sigh escaped. "Yes. He did know. But he didn't set it up. Someone else did that."

"Who?" When she remained silent, he spoke again. "Betsy? I asked you a question."

She finally returned his gaze. "It was Will Brent. But he was doing it for me, and for baby Wapi."

"I have difficulty believing Will would do *anything* for baby Wapi."

"Why not?"

"Because he's a child of the Sioux. That's all I'll tell you."

Betsy studied his face, but what she saw was the

face of Will Brent the day she'd come upon him between the buildings. She knew for certain Thad was right. Wapi's welfare was the least of Will's concern. Why, then had he agreed to set up the poker game between her and Henry?

Slowly, she nodded. "I guess you're right."

"Joseph was there. He couldn't have been entirely innocent."

"Joseph insisted on escorting me to the game and being there so he'd know I would be all right. I begged him not to tell you anything about it."

She paused at a pounding on the front door of the house.

Thad took her face in his hands quickly and those dark eyes looked down into hers.

"Stay here, until we find out who it is," he said. "Promise?"

Betsy nodded. "Promise."

A quick kiss, and he was gone.

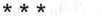

Thad automatically reached for his holster to make sure his weapon was there as he strode toward the front door. When he reached it, however, it was Joseph, with a leather sack in his hand.

"Peace, my friend."

Thad eyed him suspiciously. Normally he would have answered with an echo of '*peace*'. But it came out as, "Come in, Joseph."

"Is Betsy here?"

"She is. She's in the bedroom. What's your need to see her?"

"To give her this." Joseph held out the sack. "The men insisted she get it."

Thad didn't take the sack. Instead, he stared back at his friend. "I'll get her." When he turned to the stairway, however, Betsy was standing right behind him, wide eyed.

"Hello, Joseph."

"This is for you, Elizabeth. I know you intended to leave it, but the men insisted. You won the game; probably the first honest poker game that's been played in some time."

Betsy glanced at Thad, and sighed. "I don't feel I can accept it."

Joseph scowled. "Somehow, I knew you'd say that. Can I make a suggestion?"

Thad's gaze was still on his bride. "If you insist."

Joseph moved to the sofa and lowered himself onto it. "Please. Sit down, both of you."

Betsy was the first to comply. Eventually Thad sat

down next to her, and transferred his gaze to their guest.

Joseph looked from one to the other. "There are many things you can do with this. My suggestion, of course, is that you keep it. Since I know, you won't agree to do that, the next one is this: Put it into a fund and keep it in a safe place, and use it as you see fit. The needs of those inside the fort are many. There are also those *outside*. Use it to meet them. You could even use it for your own."

Betsy glanced at Thad before turning back to Joseph. "What do you mean? What kinds of needs?"

"You could use it for your sewing. Use it for that red cape you admired that's hanging in my window. Christmas is coming on. Use it to make gifts for those in the fort if you like." He held up his hands. "Just don't use it to meet Evaline's needs."

Betsy tilted her head, surprised. "Why?"

"Because that should be my responsibility. If you wish to make her something, do it, but I'll provide the goods for it."

"Oh. I see."

Joseph grinned. "No. It's obvious you don't. But I have my reasons. Oh, and Will Brent sent something he said needed mending." He handed her a small package wrapped in brown paper.

Thad was looking at her oddly. "Mending?"

"Yes, he asked me to mend a uniform shirt for him," she said softly.

"When?"

"On Thursday, when he offered to set the game up."

Thad opened the package and stared down at the shirt inside. A grim expression overtook his face.

"And," Joseph added, "he put some extra coins in to pay for it."

Betsy took it from him. Then she glanced up at Thad as if she was waiting on an answer. "Thad? What do you think about Joseph's idea?"

"It's your choice, sweetheart. However, I like the idea of using it to meet the needs of others."

Joseph handed the bag toward Betsy and nodded. "And here you go, Elizabeth. Yours."

Betsy stared at it with wariness, as Thad looked on. As she took it from Joseph's hand, she almost dropped it, and gasped. Thad caught it, putting his own hand under the pouch.

Joseph rose to his feet. "And now, there is just one last thing to be done. Thaddeus, come outside with me."

With a nod, Thad kissed Betsy's forehead. "Stay put, sweetheart. I won't be long."

She glanced between the two men. "Is everything all right?"

Joseph grinned. "Of course. Old friends, you know?"

Betsy wasn't so sure. Thad's expression was solemn as he followed Joseph outside and closed the door behind him.

Thad noticed the crowd that had gathered inside the fort; it seemed busier than usual. There were more soldiers present, and everyone seemed to be watching as Joseph stepped out into the middle of the yard.

Joseph's voice was quiet as he turned to face Thad. "All right. Now's the time," he said, pointing vaguely toward his jaw. "Plant it here and make it look good. People are watching."

Thad leaned back and folded his arms. "Pardon?"

Joseph grinned. "You heard me. We both have reputations to protect. I've betrayed you by helping arrange the game this afternoon instead of coming to you first. And you, my friend, have a debt to repay. You owe me."

Thad lowered his gaze to the ground, in an attempt to keep from laughing. "You're jesting."

"Nope. Not at all. Besides, I'm late for supper at Evie's. Do it. Now."

A moment later, Joseph was lying on the ground, glaring upward at Thad.

"*Good Lord*. You didn't have to plant it *that* hard."

Thad grinned back. "Yes," he said, reaching down to help his friend up, "I *did*. You all right?"

Joseph rubbed his jaw. "I'll live," he grumbled. "See you tomorrow. I'd say we've both saved our reputations. But I have to tell you. I'd give a gold piece to see you do that to Will Brent."

* * *

Betsy was pacing back and forth in front of the sofa when the door opened. Thad had returned. She eyed him carefully before saying, in a voice that oddly resembled his, a moment earlier,

"Are you all right?"

"Fine. Where did you decide to hide the pouch he brought you? No, wait. I don't want to know."

"Oh, Thad. Have you any idea how much money was in that thing?"

"No. And I don't want to know that either. It's yours, and only yours. As long as you use it to meet the needs of others, I'm satisfied. Just use it wisely, because there will be no more money coming in from poker games. Understand?"

"I understand."

"Good. Now, tell me something."

Blue eyes stared up at him. "What's that?"

He gathered her into his arms and squeezed her until she squeaked.

"I want to know," he said in a deep voice, "all about this red cape hanging in Joseph's shop window."

Before she fell asleep, Thad promised he would take her to see Joseph at the Trading Post the next morning. She was full of ideas, and he had fallen asleep listening to her chattering away about them. The last thing he remembered was her saying, "Oh, and the medicine man at Swift Eagle's tribe... what about him?"

Sleep had claimed him, however, before he'd been able to ask what she meant. But his dreams had Paytah chasing Elizabeth through the woods and chanting, shaking his shaman's tools in the air. He awakened with a fright, a vision of chasing them both toward the river vivid in his mind. The sound of the rattle faded away into thin air, and when only the darkness and quiet remained, he tightened his arms around his little bride and tried to relax once again into sleep.

Sleep, however, was elusive, and when he again opened his eyes, Betsy was nestled under his chin and snoring softly. Light was coming through the window, highlighting her body. She'd thrown off her covers and her naked form was snuggling up next to him in the morning's first light.

Thad jolted fully awake, remembering his dream only moments before. Something was not right. A dreadful sensation of being watched descended over him. Slowly, silently he covered Betsy with the quilt and moved from the bed to the window to peer through the curtains. He didn't see anyone outside, and checked under the bed and inside the wardrobe for signs of anyone there.

Then he saw it. The bedroom door was open. Thad eyed it, distinctly remembering how he'd been careful to close it the night before. A furrow crossed his brow as he realized the truth.

Someone had been inside the room.

Without dressing, he grabbed for his knife and his gun and crossed the threshold into the hallway behind the stairs.

Empty. So was the front room and the kitchen. A look into the back room indicated it too was empty.

But inside the kitchen, the backdoor was standing open. He quietly moved to it, searching the corners for other signs of visitation, but didn't see any.

When he reached the back door, however, he could hear footsteps growing fainter in the distance. Was that the sound of the shaman's rattle he heard?

He stood there as it faded completely. Then, nothing. Bolting the back door, he checked on Betsy. Frantically bounding the stairs, he made sure all was quiet before going back to her.

She had snuggled back to his side of the bed, as if seeking warmth. The desire to crawl in next to her was strong, but now was not the time to relax. Instead, he quickly dragged on his clothes and moved to lean over her.

"Elizabeth. Up with you."

She turned over, facing away from him. "Mm?"

"I'm sending you down to the tunnel."

This time she looked at him strangely. "What? *Why?*"

"Just do it. Get up. I'll help you dress. Quickly, now."

To his surprise, she obeyed, pulling on her shift and stockings. "Not the corset," he growled. "It takes too long." Helping her on with her frock and wrapping her cloak around her, he reached for the lamp and slid the opening back.

He helped her down the ladder. It took only seconds to light the lamp, and check the tunnel to make sure it was clear. When they reached the shelter, he sent her inside.

"Bolt the door and wait right here for me. I'll be back as soon as possible."

Betsy only nodded, watching with a forlorn face as she closed and bolted the door, leaving her inside with only the light of the lamp for comfort.

She waited, wondering how long it would be before he returned. Had he seen Akecheta again? Thad slept so lightly, unlike her. Where was he going? Was he in danger?

The dream she'd been having just before he awakened her recurred in her mind. Paytah had been behind her and she'd been running from him as she listened to his mumbled chants and the noise of the rattle; the same one he'd used the afternoon before when they entered the tent of Swift Eagle.

That had been the first time she'd heard the sound of

it; now, it had invaded her dreams. She thought even as she stood there, she could hear it. She held the lantern up, trying to see the entire room. All she could see, however, were the shelves filled with canned supplies and the same cots that had been there a few days before. She shivered, examining the walls and wondering if there were spiders and mice down here, or even worse; rats. Snakes?

Oh Thad, please come back.

As if in answer, the welcoming sound of his voice met her from outside the door.

"Elizabeth?"

It was Thad, and she ran toward the bolt, lifting it. Flying into his arms, she buried her face into his neck. "What happened?"

He engulfed her into his arms. "My guess is, we were visited by Paytah during the night. But I can't be sure, sweetheart. The soldiers at the gate reported hearing his rattle, even though they didn't actually see *him*."

"I... thought I heard the sound of it too, while you were gone."

His brow furrowed. "You mean—down *here*?"

She nodded. "I'm sure it probably didn't really happen, it must have been my imagination, but...."

"Stay." It was one word of command, and Betsy

closed, bolted, and leaned with her back against the door as Thad moved into the tunnel to searched it.

She moved quickly into his arms on his return. "Do you—think he might have been inside the house?"

He studied her face in the lamplight. She deserved to know. "Yes. I'm quite sure the doors were bolted, both front and back, when I came to bed last night. He might have gotten in through the windows. Unless..." He turned to glance back at the tunnel. "Here, come upstairs with me. You're shivering. I'll warm you."

She was indeed cold. Getting up the ladder was difficult, and Thad anchored his hands around her waist to help her up through the opening. He closed the trap and then shoved the wardrobe over it to block it. If Betsy questioned his action, she didn't mention it. This time, instead of undressing her, he held her close under the sheets and quilts. The lamp, he left burning.

Neither of them spoke. Finally, Betsy fell asleep in his arms, but he was thinking furiously. The very place he'd chosen to send her into might have been the place that presented the most danger for her. Why hadn't he thought of this? The next day, he would take soldiers with him and search out the tunnel to make certain his greatest fears were impossible.

Betsy, his precious little bride, had to be kept safe at all times.

* * *

Sunday...

Sunday had been an interesting day at the mission. Talk had been everywhere about the medicine man, and superstitions ran high. By the end of the service the snippets of conversation she heard included things like,

"He has the ability to make himself invisible..."

"Heard, but not seen?"

"Thad had better keep her safe. When the medicine man from the Sioux is angry with you, all sorts of bad things begin happening..."

Thad had gotten her home as quickly as possible after the morning service was over, and she'd spent the rest of the day at her sewing machine.

Suzy and Andrew spent the afternoon with them, trying to figure out ways to calm things down at the fort.

"I've never seen everyone in such a state of frenzy," Andrew remarked as Betsy served him a piece of Evie's cake. "I'm sure you and Elizabeth were the only ones here to actually hear Paytah's rattle. But from the comments at church today, you'd think everyone in the fort did."

* * *

By Monday, things seemed to have calmed somewhat. Betsy turned to Thad during breakfast.

"You promised to take me to the Trading Post today."

Thad stopped abruptly and studied her. Before he answered, he considered her request. He had indeed promised to do that, and it might be a wise idea to keep her occupied and keep her mind off what had happened during the night on Saturday.

"So I did, sweetheart. I'll take you after breakfast. Do you need to bring some of your funds with you?"

"I don't know. Perhaps? And I need you to draw some things for me on paper."

"Such as?"

"Paytah had a symbol on the back of his leather cloak when we were there. Oh, and I'd like to see the symbols that represent the tribes; the Cherokee, the Arapaho, and the Cheyenne. The Sioux, I know. And the rest of the tribes in the area? I'll need those too. Can you do that for me?"

"What are you planning to do with them?"

"I thought I might send each one a crocheted handkerchief with the symbol of their tribe embroidered on it. Would that be all right?"

"And what about Paytah?"

She sighed. "Paytah is hard. But I thought I might make him a larger piece of cloth with the symbol he was wearing Saturday when we were there. I'd really like to get started on it. It might take some time to get them all done. And I want to do Paytah's first. I thought it might soften him toward me a little."

He grinned at her oddly. "You don't ask for much, do you?"

"Please?"

"All right. Take a little of your money with you and I'll take you for a visit. And you can show me this red cape Joseph says you're so fond of. Then, I have things that must be done."

She rose, quickly moving the dishes to the sink. "What must you do?"

"I'll see if Susannah can stay with you since Evaline is off today. But I'll come and go frequently to check on you. This afternoon, I may ride over and see Swift Eagle."

Betsy stopped and whirled around to face him. "Can I go?"

He bent to plant a kiss on her forehead. "Not this

time, sweetheart. Give it another day or two before I take you with me, all right?"

"All right. But I do want to hear how baby Wapi is."

* * *

The trip to the Trading Post was satisfactory. Betsy came away with all sorts of goods for her projects. The curtains for Evie's house were now finished, and she hoped to get them hung that afternoon.

Joseph helped her pick out the materials she sought.

"Anything else?"

"No. This is all, I think."

Leaning forward, he spoke quietly.

"When will you be ready to bring the things to Evie's?"

"They're done," she whispered back. "I've hidden them in the wardrobe upstairs. Can you hang them?"

His eyes became saucers. "*Me*?"

Betsy giggled. "Perhaps not. Then Suzy and I will do it. But it'll have to be while Evie is at work."

"She works tomorrow. I'm eager to see her reaction."

"What are you whispering about?" Thad's voice

joined theirs. and Joseph jumped. "We're making secret plans," he said, grinning. "Never fear. But we might need your help."

Betsy shook her head at her husband and grinned, watching as Joseph wrapped the material in brown paper. The next time she saw Thad, however, he was standing in front of the crimson cape near the front window of the shop, running his hand over the fur that lined the hood, and nodding.

Betsy eyed him, her breath tight.

No, don't wish for things you shouldn't have. There's no reason to. The old blue one should last a few more seasons.

A moment later, however, he had walked away, and she took a deep breath and turned back to the counter.

"Ah, there you are," he said. "Did you get what you came for?"

Determined to hide her disappointment, she held out the brown packages and smiled. "Yes. Everything. It's paid for. And three of my handkerchief's sold."

"Good girl. I'm proud of you." He gave Joseph a nod and ushered her out of the shop.

When he turned left instead of right, she glanced up in confusion. "Where are you taking me?"

"To get Susannah. I don't want you spending the day alone."

Chapter Eleven

S*urprises...*

"Shh! They're coming!" Thad pulled Betsy behind him into the ally, as Joseph led Evie out of the front door and toward Thad's house. Suzy hovered behind them, trying to stifle a giggle.

Joseph leaned down into Evie's ear. "Betsy won't be there when you get there, you know. Thad promised her he'd take her to the post to pick out more goods."

"More?" Evie's voice had a surprised ring to it. "She'll be spending him into the poorhouse."

"Nah. She's got her own money."

"I hope so."

Joseph grinned at her. "Ever thought about learning to play poker?"

Suzy couldn't help it. This time, she *did* giggle.

Thad waited until the couple was inside his house before making his move to guide Betsy and Suzy toward the little hut Evie called home. "Now. Hurry."

Once inside, Betsy turned, handing Suzy an armful of folded material.

"Here, Suzy. The top one is for the kitchen window. This is for the front room and the bedroom. The rod goes through the seam *here*. I'll see if I can get the cushions sewn in while you're doing that."

They went to work. Thad kept watch at the window in case Evie returned. A moment later he glanced through back at Betsy. "How did you know what size to make them?"

She grinned. "The night while you were at your meeting, and I was pacing? I stepped it off, like you showed me in the tunnel. Then I worked out the numbers."

Thad rolled his eyes heavenward. "No one told me I married such a brilliant woman."

"And a devious one," Suzy called from the kitchen."

"Hey now," Betsy fumed as she put the first cushion in place and started sewing on the second.

* * *

By the time Betsy finished the cushions for the rocker, they were done. They stopped at the door and looked around before leaving by the back door.

Cheery yellow gingham curtains adorned the windows and cushions for the sofa and rocker, and tatted doilies crocheted with yellow thread at the edges were on the little tables and the small table at the kitchen. A tea towel sat, folded to the right of the sink. And in the bedroom, a matching doily lay on the bedside table to compliment the curtains at the window.

Thad tilted Betsy's head back and kissed her firmly. "It looks very nice, sweetheart. You and Suzy did a good job.

"Not me," Suzy said with a grin. "Betsy is definitely teaching me how to make some of these things."

Thad led them to the back door, opening it.

"Let's go"

Thad and Betsy watched again as Evie made her way home that evening, and both giggled as they peered out the front window. Suzy watched from the kitchen eagerly.

Evie stepped up on the porch and opened the door. But two steps in, she came back out. She was mumbling to herself, but none of them could understand what she was saying from so far away.

Joseph stood next to her, first opening his mouth, then closing it. Occasionally lifting his hands in the air. He was obviously puzzled at her reaction. Once in a while, he scowledd back toward the house where the three of them were.

Evie blinked, and then opened the door again; then closed it. Walking out a few steps she glanced at the surrounding houses, then back at hers.

"Oh no," Betsy murmured from her own window. "She thinks she's in the wrong house. Perhaps we'd better go over there?"

Thad laughed and took her hand. "Wait a moment, sweetheart. Let her realize what's happened. Besides," he added, "I've never seen Joseph at a loss for words before. I'm quite enjoying this."

A furious pounding on the door caused Thad to look out once again. Reaching over, he opened it. Joseph the Longhunter was standing outside, wringing his hands.

"Yes, Joseph?"

"My God. *Do* something. I've got a sobbing woman over at her house and I don't know what to do with her! What the hell do you do when a woman's crying her eyes out?"

"You hold her and try to find out what's wrong. For pity's sake, Joseph, have you never had a woman cry before?"

Joseph glared at him and raced toward Evie's house as they stood, laughing, from the window.

"Joseph needs help," Betsy giggled.

"You may be right." Thad nodded. Throwing open the door, he led the way over.

They could hear it from outside her door. Evie was still sobbing when Thad raised his fist to knock.

"Get *in* here." Joseph's voice from the inside sounded desperate. Thad pushed it open to let his wife in, and Evie turned to see them. Immediately she moved from Joseph to Betsy, throwing her arms wide.

"I love it. I adore it. No one's ever done anything like this for me before. Oh, Betsy—" she hiccupped, then stopped. "It *was* you, wasn't it?"

Betsy hugged her gently. "Well, you liked the material so much, and I thought—" She got no further. Evie began a fresh new set of tears. Joseph rolled his eyes toward the ceiling in desperation and then leveled a gaze at Thad and raised his brows.

"Good Lord."

Thad clapped him on the back. "A lesson in what *happy* tears sound like, my friend."

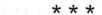

Seclusion...

Betsy hardly left the house during the next week; she stayed busy making designs on the linens she'd bought. On Thursday afternoon, she heard footfalls on the staircase and looked up to see Thad standing over her.

"You're not using your treadle."

"I know. I couldn't do this design on it. The one for Paytah had required doing it by hand. See?" She handed over the cloth she'd been working on.

Thad studied it carefully. The Sioux symbol, circled, was in the center surrounded by deep reds and oranges, and in each corner was a creature; a bear, a wolf, an eagle, and in the far lower right, a snake. In a circle near the outside were some of his shaman's tools.

"Do you think he'll like it? I didn't know about the tools, but I thought they would identify it as his."

"Oh my," he replied. "There's no doubt, sweetheart. Even if he never says so, he'll love it. I had no idea you were so talented."

She shook her head. "Not talented. Trained. Mama taught me."

He moved closer, and leaned down to kiss her forehead. "Your mother must have been very special."

Perhaps it was the fact that her hands ached after working so hard all week; the kindness in her husband's words touched her deeply. Her eyes filled with tears as she looked away with a small nod. Thad picked her up and sat down on the stool with her in his lap.

"And what did your father teach you?"

In spite of her maudlin mood, she let out a giggle.

"To play poker."

Thad watched her for a second with an incredulous expression before throwing his head back with laughter. "Oh Betsy, what am I to do with you?"

She leaned over on his chest. "I don't know. But I don't know how to change."

He kissed her, hard, before lifting her chin so she was forced to meet his eyes. "Don't," he said, kissing her again, "ever," and again, "change, my girl. I love you just the way you are."

"But I've caused you so much trouble since I've been here," she whispered, "how *can* you love me?"

Thad stared at her for a moment. "Never," he said softly, "underestimate the power of my love for you. It's strong. And it's unconditional."

Betsy sighed. "I think I don't deserve you," she whispered in his ear. "I hope I never lose you."

"You won't lose me, sweetheart," he answered in a low tone. "Are you listening?"

"I am. You said your love was strong and unconditional." Betsy's eyes flew to his.

"And," he added, "*it's eternal*."

By the beginning of the next week, she'd finished handkerchiefs for Wachiwi, Mika, and one for the chief as well, similar to the one she'd made for Paytah with the symbol of the Sioux tribe on it. For Wapi, she'd made a small blanket in Sioux colors. Thad allowed her to go with him to see baby Wapi the next time he went; his only warning was to stay quiet as much as possible during the visit, remain respectful and stay near him.

The warriors met them near the river and escorted them to the village. Betsy was glad to see them, and she knew Thad was too. The ladies near the tent were smiling; the men, curious. Chief Swift Eagle met them outside the tent.

"Welcome."

"Thank you, Swift Eagle. My wife has made and brought gifts."

Once inside the tent, Betsy glanced around. Wachiwi was humming softly on the other side to Wapi, and Mika stood in the background, watching as they entered.

Betsy reached for the package with Swift Eagle's name on it. "For you, Chief Swift Eagle," she murmured with a slight bow.

The chief opened the package and stopped, staring at her. His brown eyes traveled over the cloth, then met hers with appreciation.

"Many thanks, Bride of White Panther." When he turned to Thad, he spoke in his own language, then motioned toward his family. Thad ushered her over, where she handed gifts to the ladies and the blanket for Wapi. Wachiwi opened hers graciously; Mika had tears in her eyes. Betsy glanced down at Wapi, and gasped as she saw the change in him. In a little over a week, he had gone from being scarcely alive to being an infant who was thriving and happy. Wachiwi handed him over into Betsy's arms eagerly as the chief spoke from behind her.

"Son so...much...better. We thank you, Bride of White Panther."

Thad smiled. "She brought a gift for Paytah, too."

The chief's brow rose as she handed over the brown paper package, but he took it.

"I realize he probably hasn't forgiven me, but I want him to have it," she said softly.

As Thad interpreted for her, the chief smiled. When he spoke again, Thad turned to her.

"He says, 'Paytah is very proud.' Can you sit down and stay put while Swift Eagle and I go outside to speak?"

Betsy had the urge to scowl at him, but instead, nodded. "I'll stay." She watched as the two men left the tent, and turned back. Wachiwi had placed a blanket on the tent floor for her and patted it in an invitation for her to sit. Smiling, she cooperated. Wachiwi took Wapi back into her arms, wrapping him in the blanket Betsy had made. Smoothing her hand over it, she gave Betsy a meaningful smile.

"She says many thanks," Mika said softly.

Surprised, Betsy stared at her. "You... speak my language," she whispered.

"Yes. But Father does not know. My Akecheta—he taught me."

Before she was even aware of it, the warrior's name had brought a frown across her brow, and Mika noticed.

"No, *no*," she said, with a glance at the door of the tent. "Everyone thinks Akecheta is bad. He is not."

"No?" Betsy was aware of the disbelief in her own voice.

"No. Always good to me. Father thinks he..." She paused, and Betsy wondered if she misinterpreted the look of guilt that overcame the maiden's face. "But he did not. Not *him*."

"Then who did?" Betsy knew it was none of her business even as she asked.

"Another man," answered Mika. Turning to her mother, she smiled and interpreted.

Wachiwi nodded understanding.

"I am... so full of guilt," Mika added. "Now, Akecheta is banned from our tribe, and the guilty one is still in his place. When I woke up it was days later. Akecheta was already gone, and everyone assumed it was he who..." She stopped, misty-eyed.

"Then you must tell your father," Betsy whispered. "You should never lie to him, and Akecheta deserves to be proven innocent."

A tear made its way down Mika's cheek. "I *cannot* tell him," she said in a low voice. "He does not even know I speak your language. I feel a traitor, already."

Betsy nodded. "Mika," she whispered, "Do you love Akecheta?"

"I do love him."

Betsy put a hand over Mika's. "I can't tell you what to do, Mika. But if it were me, I would try very hard to find a way to tell him. You owe it to him. And you owe it to Akecheta. And," she added, "you owe it to yourself and your happiness."

As if she sensed Mika's distress, Wachiwi leaned toward her daughter, who spoke in her own language. Betsy assumed Mika explained what she'd said, for Wachiwi glanced at her and nodded.

"I miss Akecheta's love," Mika added. "My name... it means 'Who is like God.' It means 'God's child.' But I am not. Others tell me I am *plain*. Except Akecheta. He says I am beautiful and I am like God." She lowered her head. "But God would not do this to those he loved."

Betsy leaned forward. "No, *no*, Mika. Akecheta is right, and your name is true."

The smile Mika returned touched Betsy's heart.

The entrance of the Swift Eagle and Thad back

into the tent caused them all to turn, and no more was said. Thad approached her with an outstretched hand.

"Time to go, sweetheart."

Taking his hand, she allowed him to help her up. She glanced toward Swift Eagle, who was smiling down upon her.

"Many thanks, Bride of White Panther."

"Many thanks to you, too, sir," she said softly, nodding as Thad spoke again to the chief.

Swift Eagle gave a slight bow to her as Thad led her outside and to Wellsy.

"Warriors escort you," he said, holding up the package she'd given him for the medicine man. "I will give to Paytah."

It was as they left, Betsy caught a glimpse of Paytah heading toward the Chief's tent and wondered what his reaction would be to his gift.

But as if Thad understood her thoughts, he leaned down to her ear.

"Shh. Quiet, sweetheart."

"But—"

"Not until we get home."

Suzy came over that afternoon, demanding to know where they'd been. "I came this morning and you were gone. But Andrew said you'd gone to see Swift Eagle. What happened?"

"I took them the gifts; the blanket for Wapi, and the handkerchiefs I made for Wachiwi and Mika, and the cloths I made for Chief Swift Eagle and for Paytah." As she spoke, she felt a wave of guilt. However, she wasn't about to share what Mika had told her.

It didn't seem to matter, however. Suzy only stared at her. "You made one for Paytah too? Betsy, you must be deranged."

Betsy laughed. "Perhaps. But I guess it was sort of an appeal for forgiveness."

Suzy shook her head. "There was nothing to be forgiven for. You saved Wapi's life."

Betsy sighed. "Perhaps, but Paytah doesn't see it that way, and he's still angry with me. It's as if he thinks I tried to make his position in the tribe irrelevant. The chief says he's a very proud man." She glanced down the stairs. "But never, ever tell anyone I told you that."

Suzy turned to bestow an expression of scorn on her. "For pity's sake, who would I tell? Permelia and Cordelia? I think not. It would be all over the fort.

These two ladies amaze me with their ability to spread gossip."

Betsy was laughing now. "So, what you're saying is, don't tell them anything unless you *want* it known to everyone?"

"Exactly. I've gotten to where I duck behind a building every time I see them coming. They've finished all their canning and gardening for the summer, and they're looking for news to spread." She leaned over Betsy's shoulder.

"Now, show me what you're working on next."

* * *

Betsy realized how weary she was when Suzy left for home. She'd pulled out the materials for the Arapaho chief and his wife to work on next, but found she was too exhausted to do it. Tiptoeing halfway down the staircase, she glanced at the grandfather clock in the drawing room.

Three o'clock. Evie, was off today, and Betsy moved into the drawing room and sat down in the large chair Thad favored. It had a matching footstool, and she'd made and covered cushions for it. Leaning back, she rested her head against the cushion and closed her eyes. It wasn't long before the day began to drift away.

There was thunder in the distance; she could hear it.

Wait. Thunder?

No. *Not* thunder. Someone was pounding at the door.

"For pity's sake, hold on. I'll *get* there."

She glanced at the clock across the room from her. It said four o'clock now. She'd been asleep for a whole hour? Betsy dragged herself to her feet and stood, realizing she was still half-dazed. It took her a while to make it to the door. Jerking it open, she frowned.

"For pity's sake, Thad, I'm here. Don't be in such a hurry—" She stopped, staring. It was not Thad who stood at the door. It was a man and woman she'd never seen before. The man resembled Thad in height and size, and features. The woman next to him was smaller, with red hair parted in the middle, and a face full of freckles. Remembering her own freckles, Betsy instantly felt sorry for the woman.

When she realized she was staring, she shook herself mentally.

"Who are *you*?"

The woman's face held a distinct frown. "Is this how you greet all your guests?"

Betsy's lids were already drooping again. "No. Only the ones who awaken me out of a sound sleep. I do apologize. Please, tell me who you are before I let you in."

"Be nice, Eunice," said the man, turning to the woman with him. But to Betsy, he grinned. "And if we don't?"

"You see, it's like this. There is unrest right now in the fort. Thad would kill me if I let strangers in the house when he's not home."

"Ah, but I *am* home," said his voice, behind her.

Betsy whirled back to face him. "You came home and didn't tell me?"

"You were sleeping so peacefully, sweetheart, I didn't want to wake you." He put an arm around her and pulled her to his side. "Come in, brother. Betsy, meet my brother Patrick Bridges, and his wife Eunice. This is my darling—and *spirited* wife, Betsy. And sweetheart," he glanced down at her, "it's your turn to be nice."

"Oh dear," Betsy clapped a hand to her mouth. "I'm awake now, and I'm so *sorry*."

"You should be," Eunice's tone was short, but it was followed by Patrick's "Enough, Eunice. We arrived unannounced, and without an invitation."

Betsy felt Thad stiffen at her side, but when he

spoke, it was with graciousness. "Quite all right. I expected you, since tomorrow is my thirtieth birthday."

It was Betsy's turn to stiffen. Her shoulders back, she looked from Eunice to Patrick. "Excuse us, please." Scowling at her husband, she dragged him into the kitchen and out of sight. "You could have *told* me that," she growled in a low voice.

"Told you what?"

"That tomorrow was your thirtieth birthday! How am I supposed to know if you don't—"

"I *did* tell you, Elizabeth, the day we were married."

"But you didn't tell me it was *tomorrow*! So, this is the brother who's coming to take away your inheritance?" Her scowl increased.

"He can't do that now." He held her face in his hands, grinning. "Because I have a wife—and quite an opinionated one, at that."

Betsy couldn't help the pang of hurt that pierced her heart. He'd have to remind her it was the only reason he'd married her, especially at this time?" She looked away.

Thad turned her back to face him. "What's wrong, sweetheart?"

"You said..." she remembered sitting in his lap a

few days before and listening to him tell her how strong his love was, how unconditional; how eternal. Would he be through with her now?

Would he? Tears built at the back of her eyes as she fought to remain calm.

"Tell me," she whispered, "when you said your love for me was..."

She couldn't go on. Anger followed the hurt. Yes, he'd been good to her. Yes, he'd done everything he promised, still...

Thad pulled her closer and lifted her off her feet. Taking her into the back room where the tub was, he sat down in the chair next to it and pulled her into his lap.

"I meant every word, my darling girl. It's true, in the beginning that *was* my only reason for marriage, just as yours was the fact that you would be stranded here with no one to care for you. That's changed. Don't you dare ignore my words to you a week ago, when I held you in my arms and expressed my love for you. I meant everything I said."

"But tomorrow's your *birthday*."

"Yes. It is. How important is a birthday?"

She struggled to get out of his lap, and when she spoke, her voice had an edge to it. "Apparently it's important enough for your brother to come all the way from the east coast to be here for it," she snapped, "but not important enough for you to *tell me* about?"

He grasped her chin. "Lower your voice, young lady."

He was giving her a warning; she recognized it. Betsy lowered her eyes sadly. "All right. I'll act the dutiful wife to you while they're here."

He leaned down to plant a hard kiss on her mouth. "We'll discuss this later, sweetheart. Right now, we need to go and welcome our guests. Can you do that, and be gracious?"

Betsy pushed back the pain she felt, and nodded.

"I'll do my best." But she sounded unconvincing, and she knew it.

Thad allowed her to push against his chest until she was standing. She put on a stoic face and turned to the mirror, blinking. With a hard gulp, she grasped the doorknob and jerked it open.

Eunice was standing right outside it, Patrick behind her.

"Is there a problem?" Eunice's voice held sarcasm, and Patrick immediately pulled her away from the door.

"I do apologize for not giving you advanced notice of our visit," he said. "It was rude of us."

Betsy and Thad were barely touching, yet she

recognized the tenseness that came over him. There was a pause before he spoke.

"You need not, Patrick. You know you're always welcome here. However, I must inform you, this was not a desirable time to choose for coming."

"Oh?"

"Why not?" Eunice asked.

"There is high tension between the tribes and the soldiers at the moment, and a *lot* of it. We lost two soldiers a few weeks ago in a vicious and savage manner. And up until now, we have no proof who committed it."

Eunice put a hand to her mouth, gasping. "They were *murdered*?"

"Indeed," Thad responded. "They were. The captain and I helped bury them, and it was gruesome."

Betsy looked over her shoulder at her husband. He was making no attempt to soften what had happened. When he spoke again, he only added to it.

"Eunice, while you're here, I'll have to demand you stay in the house with Betsy. She's only allowed outside when I'm with her right now."

Eunice frowned at Patrick. "But you said I could visit the Trading Post."

Patrick gave an audible sigh of irritation. "Perhaps Thad will escort us when he has the time. And Eunice, *you* were the one who insisted on coming with me, and seeing the savages for yourself."

Betsy straightened her shoulders. "They *aren't* savages," she attested, her eyes blazing.

Patrick appeared weary, and Betsy thought better of her anger. Turning, she said softly, "Why don't both of you have a seat in the drawing room? I'll bring you something to drink until dinner is ready."

"Do you need my help, sweetheart?" Thad said, at her ear. His tone gave an unspoken request.

Please say yes.

But Betsy was still smarting, and she wasn't about to accommodate him. With a forced and quite sweet smile, she turned back to him.

"If I do, I'll call for you. You might as well visit with your brother," she said, "and enjoy yourself."

Chapter Twelve

Visitors...

Thad gave her a suspicious glance as he passed. He'd seen that look before on that adorable little face. She was up to something, and he knew it. He ushered Patrick and Eunice into the drawing room and sat with them for a while, trying his best to ignore Eunice's comments about the furniture and the curtains. Occasionally he caught a glimpse of Betsy in the kitchen, trying to get supper on the table. Obviously, she was attempting to control her expression, and he was trying to do the same. Eventually, however, it became more than he could handle, and he became so irritated at Eunice's comments, he rose to his feet and stared down at her.

"The furniture was given to me by the man who

owns the Trading Post," he said gruffly, "I admire the craftmanship in it, and my wife loves it. The place was pretty drab when Betsy came, and she made new curtains and cushions for it. Every stitch in them was sewn with love by those adorable little fingers, and whether you like them or not is irrelevant to me. *I* like them very much." He strode toward the kitchen, stopping at the doorway, and turned back. "And if it disturbs you to sit on them, you may stand."

Betsy couldn't help the giggle that erupted from her. She turned away so her visitors were unable to see her face. Thad wandered into the kitchen with an annoyed stride and reached for her, tilting her back in his arms and kissing her in full sight of his brother and his wife.

"I take back what I said," he whispered into her ear. "Graciousness evidently isn't one of my strengths."

"Oh, but I disagree. I think your comment about my sewing is the loveliest one I've ever heard." She waved her fingers at him, grinning. "I never quite thought of them as adorable, though."

"To me they are. And I generally can be nice, but not when someone criticizes the one who has my heart." He closed his eyes briefly. Opening them a moment later, he gathered her to him. Another kiss followed the first, and he gave her a pat, sending her toward the sink.

Supper went well. The cornbread and beans Evie had made the day before were delicious. Betsy smeared the cornbread liberally with butter. After supper Thad made coffee, and Betsy served it with large slices of marbled cake for dessert, sprinkled with cinnamon and sugar.

Patrick smiled at Betsy as he finished swallowing the last of the cake. "Betsy, where did you learn to cook like this?"

Betsy paused only briefly. It was nice of Patrick to make an effort. She grinned back at him.

"Oh, this wasn't *my* cooking. We have a lady who comes a few days a week. She does most of the cooking. She's trying to teach me, but honestly, I feel as if I'm a failure. I do better at sewing and needlework."

It was the first time she'd seen Eunice smile, and it wasn't a very cordial one. Betsy chose to ignore it, adding, "I'm afraid if you stay very long, you'll regret it." She sent a grin Thad's way, but he reached over and took her hand in his.

"I'm staying, sweetheart," he remarked, "and I don't regret it at *all*."

Betsy found herself studying her husband's face.

He looked as if he meant every word, and she felt her eyes grow misty.

Patrick, watching them as they locked eyes with each other, remained quiet. Eunice, however, picked up her dishes and carried them to the sink. "Well," she remarked, "Since Betsy doesn't know how to do anything, I suppose I'll have to wash the dishes."

"Oh, I do that very well," Betsy chirped. "You can go sit down in the drawing room if you like. And feel free to criticize."

Sputtering, Eunice left the dishes in the sink and disappeared into the drawing room. Patrick followed, whispering in her ear.

"Be nice, Eunice. We're their guests, remember?"

It *was* overheard, however, and Thad bent down to Betsy. "I suppose we both need to be nice. And sweetheart, when you do receive a compliment, it isn't necessary to confess you don't know how to do something."

Betsy raised up on her tiptoes to give him a brief kiss on the cheek, and whispered in his ear. "You've already told me what a terrible liar I am. And I believe you've yet to teach me how to '*do it properly*'."

Thad rolled his eyes. "I suppose I deserved that one," he muttered under his breath. With one last solemn glance, he strode into the drawing room, leaving Betsy to finish washing and drying the dishes.

She took her time, lingering over them. When she entered the drawing room at last, however, she glanced at Eunice. "I'm going upstairs to the sewing room. Would you like to join me?"

The expression on Eunice's face was uncertain. "Perhaps."

"Take an extra lamp with you, sweetheart." Thad reminded her. Betsy retrieved one from the kitchen, lighting it.

"The days are getting short," she announced as they climbed upward. "Always have a lantern with you. And I meant to tell you, any time you'd like to have a bath, we'll be glad to prepare the tub."

Eunice stared back at her. "You have running water?"

Betsy laughed. "No, but Thad and the soldiers bring water from the river and we have a stove to heat it with. The tub is in the back room off the kitchen. And there's chamomile soap to bathe with, and rosemary scented tea to rinse your hair with."

"Oh," Eunice considered her words. "That sounds like it would be tolerable."

"Very nice, actually." Betsy gave her a sly grin. "Especially when your husband is there to wash your hair for you." Adding a giggle, she flounced on up the stairs with a grin on her face, leaving Eunice staring after her with her mouth open.

For a moment Betsy thought Eunice wasn't going to follow, but eventually she did show at the top of the stairs. Pulling the stool out from under the sewing table, Betsy shoved it in her direction and sat down in the rocker by the window.

There was a knock on the front door, and voices below. Betsy recognized Suzy's merry voice, and smiled; at least she wouldn't have to spend the entire evening trapped up here with Eunice.

A moment later Suzy appeared with Thad behind her, carrying up one of the kitchen chairs.

"Oh Suzy, I can't tell you how good it is to see you," Betsy hugged her friend. "Suzy, this is Eunice, my... sister-in-law." She nearly choked on the words, but managed to get them out.

Suzy glanced back and forth between Betsy and Eunice, finally answering.

"I see. Eunice, it's nice to meet you. Betsy, it's good to see you too, my friend. Have you made any progress since I left this afternoon?"

Betsy stared back at her. She wasn't about to produce the jacket she'd been making for Thad. If Eunice was to criticize it, Betsy thought she might just throw her down the stairs.

But Eunice was eying Suzy curiously. "How is it that you're allowed to come visiting at night when there is unrest among the tribes?"

"Because," Suzy leaned forward, "my husband is right downstairs. He escorted me. Betsy, have you shown her what you're working on?"

"Not yet. This is one of them." Betsy pulled out the drawing she had intended to turn into needlework, and the handkerchief she'd begun. "And *this*."

"A flower?"

"It's called *prairie larkspur*. I got the thread and the linen from Joseph the Longhunter, who owns the Trading Post. He manages to get in some lovely colors. And *this* one," she added, taking out another one, "is called *butterfly weed*. Joseph got this thread color for me, too. There are more, but I haven't begun working on them yet. I hope you do get to go to the Trading Post while you're here. They have some wonderful things there."

"What are you going to do with these?"

Betsy smiled. "I'm putting these in the Trading Post. I've already sent some to the wives of the tribal chiefs."

"Why?" Eunice's question was honest, and Betsy answered.

"Because gifts are a way of encouraging peace between the two people; them, and us."

"Patrick says they're savages."

Betsy stared at her. "Patrick," she said in a low voice, "is *wrong*. They are people, just like us, with families, wives and little children. He should *meet* some of them before passing judgement on them."

"You sound like you *like* them." Eunice sounded accusatory, and Betsy straightened her shoulders.

"I *do* like them. I like them *very much*."

"And," Suzy added in a whisper behind them, "if I were you, I'd be very careful what I say, even in the fort. The walls may have ears."

Betsy knew exactly what she meant. The memory of the shaman's rattle was still fresh in her mind.

Eunice's eyes widened. But for a change, she remained silent.

Betsy celebrated Thad's birthday the next day with a cake she had helped Evie bake that afternoon. Evie's buttercream icing coated it thickly, and tasted wonderful. Joseph, Father O'Leary, and Andrew and Suzy were there.

Among the birthday wishes, Betsy presented her

husband with the warm jacket she'd made from material at the post Joseph had sold her. Joseph gave him a warm cap for the winter, Andrew a knife he'd obtained from the Trading Post as well, and Susannah brought a tray of his favorite cookies and a warm scarf. Even the twins had stopped by earlier in the day and left jars of bread and butter pickles they'd made from the garden that year.

"We knew you liked these," Cordelia said brightly, bobbing up and down. "Didn't we, Permelia?"

"Yes! We knew indeed."

Betsy felt dizzy, watching them as they bounced. When she recovered, she spoke. "Can you possibly stay for dinner?"

The movement changed to a side to side motion as they declined. "Perhaps a later time. But do try some of these, Betsy," Cordelia said, motioning toward the big jars they'd left on the table. "If you like them, Permelia and I will come next year and share our secret recipe."

"Oh my. I won't let you forget that," Betsy grinned as she hugged each of them and thanked them before they left.

The chatter was loud and the room full of cheers when they finished eating. Thad turned to Betsy and kissed her thoroughly in front of the crowd while Joseph and Andrew whistled.

"Thank you, sweetheart. This has been a wonderful birthday."

Betsy helped Evie wash and dry the dishes as the crowd migrated to the drawing room. They hadn't been there long, however, when Patrick turned to Thad.

"I still haven't seen a copy of your marriage certificate, brother."

"I have." Joseph leveled a gaze at him.

"I have too," Andrew added. "In fact, Suzy and I were witnesses. I signed it."

"And I performed the ceremony," Father O'Leary tossed in a large grin. "I signed it too."

"You don't understand," Thad said firmly. "This is my brother. He'll want to see it." Rising, he disappeared into the bedroom and appeared a moment later with it in his hand.

Overhearing the conversation, Betsy watched as her husband returned from the bedroom. "Here it is, Patrick," he said, handing it over.

Patrick took it, looking slightly sheepish, and examined it closely. It was a moment before he handed it back. "It looks authentic. What can I say, brother? You win."

Thad stared at him. "It isn't a contest, Patrick. I was blessed enough to find this young lady, that's all."

He chuckled, glancing into the kitchen at Betsy. "Even though she did try hard to outrun me."

She approached him, wrapping her arms around him and leaning her head over on his shoulder. "Oh Thad. I do love you so."

Applause went through the room at her words, and Thad hugged her tightly. It wasn't until after the cheers ended that Betsy noticed Eunice had gotten up and left the room, leaving Patrick there alone.

Eunice was at the top of the stairs when they heard it; an Indian war cry seared through the air of the fort, causing panic in everyone present.

Thad took Betsy tighter in his arms. "Get the ladies, sweetheart. Go upstairs and down through the tunnel. I'll be there to get you as soon as possible. Don't forget the lantern, but don't light it until the trap is shut."

Betsy didn't argue. She noticed Evie had the kitchen lantern in her hand, and she made sure Suzy and Evie ran upstairs ahead of her. Eunice was waiting at the top, still as stone. Betsy ran into the closet and grabbed the lantern from its hiding place along with the box of long matches, and opened the trap door.

"Go now," she whispered to the others, "*quietly*." Running back toward Eunice, she took the girl by the shoulders. "Hurry, Eunice. Follow the others, and be as quiet as you can."

But Eunice's face was angry. "I don't believe you. I heard what you said the other night when you and Thad were in the back room. You said you would act the part until we were gone."

Betsy panicked. "We can talk about this later, but if you stay here you may end up in danger. Please, *hurry*!"

Betsy thought for a moment Eunice would refuse, but soon she moved. When she saw the darkness of the tunnel below, however, she balked.

"It—it's *black down there*."

"I'll light the lamp after we close the trap," Betsy whispered. "Just *go*!"

Eunice paused, but only for a few seconds. At Betsy's urgent whisper, she finally followed the others down.

Holding onto the unlit lamp with trembling fingers, Betsy climbed down and placed it on the hook, closing the trap. A moment later, there was light as she struck the match and lit the lantern. A sigh of relief escaped from the others as their darkness was replaced with light. "This way," she said, thankful she could remember the direction Thad had showed her. Evie was still carrying her lamp, but had not yet lit it.

As they reached the opening, Betsy held out her lamp to Evie. "Light yours now," she whispered, "I can't stay."

Evie's face grew grim. "What are you going to do? Betsy, you can't—"

"Just do it!" Betsy whispered, "The twins should be there by now, and the other ladies from the fort. And Suzy, I'm depending on you to keep everyone calm." When Suzy studied her face, she mouthed, "especially Eunice."

Suzy was shaking her head. "Betsy, Thad will kill you when he finds out you didn't stay inside the shelter."

"I know, but he may need me more than you all do. It's *you* they need here."

"But—"

Betsy kissed her cheek and retrieved her lantern. Scurrying back through the tunnel in the opposite direction, she began climbing the ladder upward. The light from the lamp found the hook on the wall, and she hung it there, and reached upward to the trap, resting one hand on knob.

With a quick breath, she blew the lamp out.

"Dear God, please, keep Thad safe," she prayed, "and everyone else."

Slowly and silently, she slid the trap back.

* * *

Slowly, *slowly*, she raised her head far enough above the opening in the floor to glance around the room.

Silence. There was still enough light to see well, and Betsy waited a few more seconds, listening.

Nothing.

It was hard to make her feet move as she set the lantern down and climbed out of the opening. The closing of the trap sounded like thunder to her, and she closed her eyes.

Finally, satisfied there was no one in the upstairs floor, she rose to her feet and moved to the sewing room. It too, was quiet and empty.

Where was Thad?

Betsy lowered herself to her belly at the top of the stairs, and leaned forward, watching the lower floor. It was several long moments before she was convinced there was no one there. Thad was likely with Andrew, Joseph and Father O'Leary. Where was Patrick? Was he with them too?

At least she was not having to deal with Eunice at the moment. That was a blessing. She rose silently, and tiptoed down the staircase, satisfied she wasn't making any noise as she reached the bottom. Moving to the front window, she carefully peeked out to see what was happening.

There was no sign of anyone. Where were they?

Suddenly she saw a shadow crossing the yard of the fort. It was headed her way, and she ducked into the kitchen and let herself out the back door, closing it softly.

There was still enough light to see, and for that she was thankful. Peeking around the side of the house, she was glad when only emptiness met her gaze. Carefully she moved to the back of the next building.

She'd crossed five or six of the buildings when she realized there was someone behind her, and her heart stopped.

Oh God. Please don't let it be Thad.

Turning silently, she gave off a quiet breath of relief when she saw Lt. Will Brent standing behind her, grinning.

"Lieutenant Brent," she whispered. "Where's Thad?"

"I know where he is. Aren't you supposed to be hidden away in the tunnel?"

Betsy trembled. She wasn't sure how to answer. Was Brent supposed to know about the tunnels?

Feeling silly, suddenly, she realized of course he

probably knew about them. All the soldiers probably did.

"I... need to talk to him."

"I'm not so sure about this. But I'll take you. Thad nearly beat me to a pulp when he found out I helped arrange the poker game with Henry, you know. You'll owe me."

"Please, just take me to him?"

He sighed. "All right. Come with me."

He reached for Betsy's hand, drawing her in front of him; an odd thing for a soldier to do, she thought. Thad always put her behind him when there was danger—

Betsy's thoughts halted suddenly as a large hand was clapped over her mouth. She didn't even have a chance to scream before a sweet-smelling cloth covered her nose and mouth, and the same smell permeated the air, filling her lungs.

It didn't happen all at once; her breath eventually became short; her ability to struggle was hindered even though she tried her best. The last thing she remembered was Brent's deep voice speaking, but it wasn't to *her*.

"Here, take her. Put her in the tent and watch her until I get there. For *now*."

Chapter Thirteen

Captured...

There were several voices in the room. Betsy could hear them, but she was too groggy to open her eyes.

No, that's wrong. There are only two of them.

One belonged to Brent. The other was familiar; she'd heard it before, but something about it was different. Whereas before she'd only heard his voice in broken English, now he was speaking her language fluently.

A soft female voice from the past wafted through her mind; a memory from the past few days. And another voice; her own.

You speak my language.

My Akecheta—he taught me...

Now, she knew whose voice she heard.

Akecheta!

Her eyes flew open, but neither of the men were looking at her, and she closed them again, hoping they wouldn't realize she was awake.

"What do you plan to do with her?" Akecheta's voice.

There was a silence. A moment later, Betsy heard Brent's answer.

"Kill her."

Betsy fought the chill that descended over her. But as soon as Brent spoke, the warrior spoke again.

"Why? What has she done? Why kill someone who is innocent?"

Brent's voice was evil. "Did I need a reason to dispose of Mose and James? No. She'll be even easier. Besides," he added, "it won't be me who kills her. It will be *you*."

There was a rustling sound. Then Brent spoke again. "I'll be back shortly. And I want her awake when you do it. I want Thad to hear her screams in his dreams when he sleeps at night." He paused. "Don't dispose of her until I return and give the order."

Akecheta answered, but Betsy heard anger in his voice this time. "*You* do not give *me* orders."

There was a long silence before Brent spoke.

"We'll see."

Again, there was a rustling sound followed by silence. Betsy was quiet. But she needed to speak with Akecheta, and this might be her only chance. After all, Mika had spoken well of him, hadn't she?

Slowly, she opened her eyes. He was still sitting as he had been before, but this time he was watching her. When he became aware of her wakeful state, he put a finger to his lips. "Don't scream," he said in a low voice.

He didn't appear threatening. Betsy watched him, studying his features. Finally, she dredged up the courage to speak.

"You speak my language very well. I could hear you as I awakened."

"Yes." He gave no reason, only an acknowledgement. "Better others do not know. If I knew you were awake, I would have stayed silent."

"Mika speaks highly of you," she whispered. "Can I trust what she says to be true?"

Akecheta looked away, as a gentle smile crossed his face, followed by an expression she could only interpret as betrayal. "My Mika always speaks truth. Except," he added, "when it comes to my defense."

"But we talked about that," Betsy said softly, glancing around the empty tent, and wondering when

Brent would come back. "I encouraged her to tell her father the truth about you."

Akecheta leaned forward. "Did she tell you who assaulted her?"

Betsy shook her head. "No, she didn't. But she had tears in her eyes when she said," she searched her memory from a few days ago. Then she looked up at him. "She said, 'Now Akecheta is banned from our tribe, and the guilty one is still in his place...'" Struggling to sit up, she fought the dizziness and nausea that plagued her and steadied herself on the floor of the tent. "At first," she added, "I thought she meant the guilty one was in *your* place, and I thought perhaps it was another warrior. But..." She turned to Akecheta. "Perhaps she *didn't*."

The warrior shook his head, confused, and Betsy continued. "Perhaps she meant the guilty one was still in the place he'd always been. Akecheta, if that's true, she could have meant the guilty man was another warrior, or even a..." Her voice dropped to a whisper, and her face became grim. "Even a *soldier*. Oh dear God. That would mean *war*." She halted, realizing her words could be interpreted as inciting the Sioux to war with the white men.

Akecheta moved closer, and halted. "Yes. You understand. I see."

Betsy reached out to him. "Akecheta, I..." she licked her lips nervously. "I begged her to tell her father you didn't do it. And to tell him who *did*."

The warrior before her rose to his feet and began pacing. "Then we must prepare for war," he said. "Chief Swift Eagle is wise. But also, is protective of family. It was better for me to accept blame than to have battle between whites and Sioux."

Betsy frowned. "But you're not guilty," she insisted. "Another thing I overheard as I woke up," she said, lowering her voice even more. "Brent said he killed Mose and James. I heard him, before he left. He said he would come back, and then he expected you to kill *me*." Her voice took on a tone of fright. "Will you, Akecheta? Kill me?"

He dropped to his knees before her. "I am a warrior for our tribe, Bride of White Panther. I do not kill innocent women and children. He meant he would come back and kill you himself. And then he would tell others it was me."

Betsy wasn't sure if her relief was well-founded. "Then what can we do?" She blinked, frowning.

Akecheta stared at her. "Brent thinks nothing of committing murder. Thad already knows. Do not worry. White Panther knows."

"He—he does?"

"I have told him. He already suspected. And he said be patient."

Akecheta held out a hand. Betsy stared at it, uncertain whether to take it or not. When he spoke again, his voice was quiet.

"Mika speaks truth. You *can* trust me. Come."

His hand felt strong as she placed hers in it and followed him to the door. He turned to her as they reached it and gave her a small push out of sight. "Stay and listen. Brent is speaking. I want to see who is *listening.*"

Betsy hovered just inside, waiting. Outside, she could hear the Lieutenant. His voice was loud and authoritative. Most of all, it was accusatory.

"Listen. I'm telling you the truth. It wasn't any of the tribes who killed those two soldiers. It was Akecheta, and he was acting *alone.*"

Betsy gave a quiet gasp as Brent continued to shout his accusations. He tried to place the blame for the soldiers on the man in front of her, and the warrior again put a finger to his lips. She sneaked out from behind her hiding place, trying to see what was happening. But when Brent turned toward the tent where they stood, she stepped back, unsure what to do.

Brent's voice became louder, suddenly. "Not only

is he guilty, he plans to kill Betsy, the new bride of Thaddeus Bridges, whom you know as White Panther. And there," he shouted, pointing, "he *is*, the vicious man you seek!"

The crowd, both Indian and white, was becoming militant, and Betsy could no longer keep quiet. Akecheta seemed to show no fear, but he turned to push her back further, away from the possible danger.

"*No.*" It was already out of her mouth. She could not allow an innocent man to be blamed if she could prevent it. Warriors were drawing their arrows from their quivers and aiming.

"*No!*" She ducked under Akecheta's arm and swiftly moved in front of him, throwing her arms wide in an effort to protect him. The warrior attempted to put her behind him, but she refused to move.

"Stop!" she shouted at the top of her lungs. "Put away your weapons! Akecheta is *not* guilty! Will Brent kidnapped me. I heard him admit inside this tent that *he* was the one who killed Mose and James! And he planned to kill me himself and blame it on Akecheta."

Betsy could see Thad, who immediately began racing toward her. The look on his face was almost apoplectic. But as he came closer, Betsy feared the crowd would attack him because he was in the way.

"No, Thad. Stop!"

He did *not* stop. He put himself directly in harm's way, turning to face the confused crowd. Betsy was amazed at the calmness of his voice as he spoke. She was also thankful the crowd seemed to listen carefully to him.

"Everyone," he said, "stop for a moment and listen to me. My wife speaks truth. The night Mose and James were killed, I was the first to reach their bodies. Andrew and Joseph were with me. All of us were uncertain who the murderer was, but all of us did *not* think it was done by any of you from the tribes. We know now, who did it."

Brent's face held an evil grin as he stared back, seeming sure of himself. "You have no proof of anything, Bridges." His voice sounded as evil as his face appeared." And what evidence do you have against me? The opinion of your *wife*?" He threw back his head and laughed.

Thad waited until he finished before turning to the crowd. Standing between Brent and Akecheta who had finally managed to shove Betsy behind him, he took a step closer to the lieutenant and centered those eyes of steel on him.

Thad's shoulders were straight as he faced the crowd.

"*This*." He reached into his pocket and pulled out

a small piece that was gold and shiny, and held it up in front of Brent. "I believe is *yours*."

Brent's face paled. He lunged forward to grab for the piece held in Thad's hand. At the same instant, Thad tossed it high in the air toward Andrew. The captain deftly caught it.

Andrew cocked his head toward Thad. "I'd love to know where you got this. And why you didn't tell me." He held it up for everyone to see, and moved his gaze to Brent. Several soldiers now had Brent restrained, refusing to release him.

"I found it," Thad answered, "clutched in Mose's right hand the night we buried him. Apparently, he didn't give up without a fight. The next night at the meeting I looked around and examined each soldier's uniform. Only one was missing a badge. Lieutenant Will Brent." He paused for a few seconds before continuing.

"A few days ago, he asked that Betsy would mend one of his uniforms, in the exact spot where he usually wears the badge. I kept quiet, because I needed more evidence before accusing one of the soldiers and perhaps causing war between us."

Andrew's gaze altered between the piece in his hand, and the soldier standing before him who had been the next in the line of command. His face became grave. "The badge of Lieutenant Will Brent." Leveling a gaze at Brent, he added, "What have you to say for yourself?"

It was at that exact moment, Brent managed to free one arm. He pulled a pistol from his gun belt and pointed it directly at Thad, who stood in front of Akecheta. The warrior flung Betsy inside the tent, but she didn't stay long. Up on her feet suddenly and moving toward the opening, she was just in time to hear a shout from Brent.

"They lie! They *all* lie!"

It happened so fast, Betsy didn't know where to look. As Will drew back his arm to shoot, the air erupted with shouts and war cries. Arrows seemed to come from everywhere, along with the deafening sound of gunfire. Betsy ran through the opening of the tent, sobbing out Thad's name and expecting to see blood pouring from his chest, but Akecheta had caught her before she reached her husband.

"No, let me *go*!"

She managed to get away, darting around him. Bolting like lightning toward her husband, she sobbed out his name and threw herself into his arms.

"*Thad!*"

"Shh. Quiet, sweetheart." His voice was gruff, "I'm all right."

Betsy ran her hand down his shirt, as if to reassure herself he was really unharmed. His face was next. His expression became gentle as he took her in his arms, whispering calming words to her and rocking her gently.

"Quiet, my love," he whispered as she closed her eyes and melted into his embrace.

Her shoulders drooped as she finally opened her eyes, taking in the scene around her. There was only silence.

Time seemed to stand still.

Will Brent lay dead on the ground, his body full of more arrows than she could count. Betsy turned her face into Thad's neck, unable to take in the gruesome scene, and he pressed her to him, turning her away from it.

"Oh, *dear God*," she whispered. But her small utterance seemed to go unheard. Thad drew her even closer, whispering to her.

When she dared survey the scene again, the first person she saw was Swift Eagle, holding the gold badge of Will Brent in his hand. His eyes full of hatred, he held out the badge and spit on it before tossing it to the ground in disgust. Moving forward, he ground it into the dust before turning away.

One by one, the chieftains and warriors began to do the same.

It was when they finished and moved back to their own tribes that Swift Eagle caught sight of Akecheta and approached, his countenance dark and forbidding.

"Akecheta *still* banned from Sioux tribe. Responsible for daughter's beating." His face was red, and his expression fiery.

"No, father! *No!*" Mika and Wachiwi appeared from the crowd. Mika ran to her father, standing between him and Akecheta. "It *wasn't* Akecheta!"

Swift Eagle halted abruptly, turning back and staring between his wife and his daughter. "Speak," he commanded.

Wachiwi stepped forward, uttering something Betsy was unable to understand, and the chief turned to face Mika. Betsy watched her hopefully.

Courage, Mika. Tell him the truth.

Mika was having difficulty as she raised her eyes to her father's. "I was out in the forest one day and came across a man—a soldier. At first, I thought he was a kind man. But then..." She choked on a sob before speaking again. "My head hurt so bad. I could hear Akecheta's voice growing closer as I lost... and the soldier sounded far away, and I..." She shook her head. "When I awakened, Akecheta had already been banned."

Betsy expected the chief to explode. But silence reined as everyone in the crowd looked on. When Swift Eagle spoke, his voice to his daughter was gentle.

"Why?" he asked. "Why not speak before now?"

Mika approached, putting a hand to her father's cheek. "I feared becoming the cause of war between us and the white man. You have always taught me to be wise when making decisions. But Betsy told me I should talk to you, and tell the truth."

Swift Eagle stepped around her and continued to approach Akecheta. "This is true?"

Akecheta's voice was humble. "She speaks the truth."

"But you," the chief spoke in astonishment, "you allow us to think it was *you*."

"The truth would come to light." Akecheta faced him solemnly. "And it has. *This* day."

Chief Swift Eagle dropped his gaze.

"You use my words," he said quietly.

Akecheta answered, his voice thoughtful.

"*Wise* words, my chief."

Swift Eagle's head jerked upward at the address, and Betsy wondered what he was thinking. A long moment passed between them. The chief was staring at the body of Will Brent, and occasionally moved his gaze to the badge in the dirt next to Brent's body.

Holding out one hand to Mika and motioning toward Akecheta as well, he nodded.

"Justice done. But not all," he said. "Come. We talk."

Before he reached the tent, however, he turned back. His voice kind, he smiled, first at Thad, then at Betsy.

"Again, Bride of White Panther. *Thank* you," he said.

* * *

Betsy watched as they all disappeared into the Chief's tent. However, as she looked upward, other tribes were closing in on them, asking questions in their own tongues. Thad sat down on a tree stump and began answering each in their own language, patiently.

Betsy watched her husband with awe. He was a truly amazing man, not only to be able to speak the languages of each tribe, but to keep a calmness of spirit about him. He reached out to each one with an attitude of peacefulness and respect as he xplained what had happened.

She sat down, leaning against the stump, and smiled up at him as he spoke, and occasionally he gave her a wink in return.

Eventually, the crowd began to disperse. Thad noticed Betsy's weariness and reached down, drawing her into his lap.

Her lids began to droop. Just before they closed, however, she caught sight of Patrick on the outskirts of the crowd, watching.

His face held as much awe and respect as she felt hers must.

When she opened her eyes again, she was lying in her own bedroom. It was dark, and the lamp was lit. Thad was lying behind her and she was engulfed in his arms as he watched her, his expression gentle. But when he spoke, his voice was deep.

"You," he said, "are in *so* much trouble, young lady."

She knew her expression was crestfallen. "Oh," was all she said, before he leaned forward, kissing her temple.

"We'll talk about this tomorrow."

She let her lids close again. "Tomorrow," she whispered. A moment later, however, her eyes flew open again. "The ladies! Suzy and Evie and Cordelia and Permelia and Eunice—"

"They're all back home now, sweetheart. Patrick and Eunice are upstairs. No worries."

"But—"

"Shh. Sleep now. You've been heroic enough for one day."

She squinted up at him. "I have?"

His smile was endearing. "Yes. Quite enough. Now, *tomorrow*, we'll discuss obedience."

It was all she heard before her eyes closed.

Chapter Fourteen

Waiting...

Betsy had been awakened during the night for intense lovemaking, and she adored every second of it although she found herself surprised. Thad seemed to have a storm inside him, and it was as if each of them attempted to find release through wildness; Betsy wondered if it was due to what they'd been through the day before.

When she awakened the next morning, however, the smell of breakfast had wafted into the room.

What time was it?

Just then, the gong of the grandfather clock in the living room sounded.

Ten o'clock.

"Ten!" Betsy sat straight up, reaching over to Thad's side of the bed only to find it was cool.

Why hadn't he awakened her?

Racing for the wardrobe, she dressed quickly and opened the door. The house was empty but for Evie, who was milling about in the kitchen. A place was set for one, where she usually sat.

"I was hoping it would wake you up. Thad left early. He said to let you sleep; you'd been through hell and back yesterday." Evie smiled. "Those were his words, not mine, mind you."

"I'm disappointed," Betsy answered, a frown working its way across her brow. "I thought he'd wake me."

Was she disappointed? *Really*? Betsy felt her face grow hot as she remembered the last thing he'd said to her as she'd fallen asleep the night before. They would be having a discussion today...

About obedience.

Evie, however, set a cup of coffee down next to her plate, along with a glass of fresh milk. Pouring herself a cup, lowered herself into the chair next to Betsy.

"Thad told me about what happened yesterday.

He told me how you jumped in front of the warrior and tried to protect him from the Lieutenant. What made you do that?

Betsy stared at her. "I didn't think about it. I only knew that he was innocent, and he was in danger of being slaughtered right before my eyes. He's the hero, Evie, not me."

Evie laughed. "Well, your Thad seems to think otherwise. But he doesn't seem to know whether to kiss you or spank you."

Betsy sighed, glancing around the empty house. "I just noticed. Patrick and Eunice don't seem to be here. Are they still asleep?"

Evie leaned forward. "They left early this morning. And you didn't hear it from me, but I for one am *thrilled* they're gone. I did feed them before they left, but Eunice complained the whole time about the canned food they ate yesterday while they were in the shelter. Of course, she complained then, too."

Betsy sighed. "I'm so sorry."

"Permelia said," Evie began bouncing up and down to imitate the twins and their voices. "You should be thankful, my dear. When we first came, there *was* no shelter here. We were just at the mercy of whoever came after us." Evie stopped bouncing, and looked over her shoulder, as Permelia would have. Then began bouncing again. "Weren't we, Cordelia?"

Betsy began giggling. "You do that so well, Evie."

"And Cordelia said," Evie began bouncing again, adding in a high-pitched voice, "Why yes, Permelia. Yes, we *were*."

Betsy was hooting with laughter by the time she finished. "And what happened then?"

Evie shook her head. "Then Eunice wanted to know why she wasn't allowed to go with you instead of having to wait in that dark, dank room."

Betsy laughed. "Did she? Oh my. Perhaps Patrick should have just left her in there." Realizing what she'd said, she clapped her hand to her mouth, but Evie was laughing along with her.

"I won't tell. I promise." Evie's voice was low. "Because I'd be in trouble too, for I agree with you." She leaned forward, lowering her voice even further. "*Completely*. I don't know how he manages to live with her. Oh! That does remind me. She left a note for you. Let me get it." She disappeared for a moment; when she returned, there was a pink envelope in her hand.

"From Eunice?"

Evie nodded. "From the queen herself. But I didn't say that either." She handed it over as Betsy giggled.

Neat script adorned the envelope, and inside was a folded page.

Dearest sister-in-law,

Betsy stopped. "Dearest? Is she being sarcastic?"

Evie shook her head, and Betsy read on.

I do owe you a big apology. Patrick explained last night how you'd been kidnapped yesterday and how you managed to stop a war from happening. He said you jumped in front of an innocent man while the Indians had drawn their arrows, and the soldiers had drawn their guns on him.

I am speechless at your courage, dear Betsy. I never could have done that.

You are an amazing woman, and it is a story I will tell my children and grandchildren.

Thad must be extremely proud of you...

As am I.

Eunice

. . .

Betsy stared at the note, then at Evie. "Oh my," she said softly. "Oh *my*."

* * *

The pounding on the door caused her to run to unbolt it. Thad stood outside and took her hand, leading her out of the house toward him. He removed his jacket and wrapped it around her shoulders when the fierce wind began to blow her hair back from her face.

"There are a few people who wish to speak to you." he said.

Betsy's gaze roamed over the crowd standing just outside the house. Whites and Natives alike stood there. She gulped.

"A *few*?"

Thad's mouth lifted on one side in a smile. "Look, sweetheart," he said softly.

Chief Swift Eagle was the first to step out into view. "You are friend to Sioux, Bride of White Panther. You have courage. Bravery. Heart. You bring my son back to us. You bring Akecheta back to us. We thank you."

Betsy stared at him, uncertain what to say. Seconds

later, Wachiwi appeared beside her husband with a sleeping baby Wapi in her arms. But her language was in Sioux, and Betsy was unable to understand it. Akecheta stepped up to interpret, Mika next to him.

As Wachiwi finished speaking, the chief turned to the warrior quietly. Akecheta nodded respectfully toward Betsy. "Wachiwi says, 'You gave me my son back from the dead. I cannot thank you enough. Even though you had to win the goat to bring him back to us.'"

There was a slight chuckle through the crowd who had gathered, and Betsy gave Thad a glance of uneasiness. He was still grinning at her, however, and gathered her tightly to his side.

Mika was next.

"I lived in the shadow of guilt and fear too long. You gave me courage," she said softly, "because you *showed* courage when you ran in front of my Akecheta to save him. Then, I knew. I *knew* I could do it."

Akecheta put his arms around Mika, but spoke to Betsy. "Bride of White Panther," he stood tall and strong as he spoke, "You gave me life again. Life *again* with my Mika. Life serving my *chief*. Life with my people. And life again with my father."

Betsy stared. "Father?" she whispered.

Akecheta smiled, and turned to another of the

tribe, who stood behind him. When the man stepped forward, Betsy gasped.

It was Paytah.

He was wearing the linen cloth Betsy had made for him over his shoulders. His face held, not a smile, but a gentleness she hadn't seen on him before. She knew it was one she would never forget. Nodding toward her, he reached out, resting a hand on Akecheta's shoulder.

"Paytah." Akecheta said quietly. "*My father*."

Betsy understood, then, as the warrior continued.

"What more can a warrior ask? Thank you."

Betsy glanced at Chief Swift Eagle, who had his head bowed. Was that a tear she saw working its way down his cheek? She swallowed hard, as tears continued to form in her own eyes and threatened to spill over.

Thad nudged her as someone else stepped out into the opening and spoke in a different tongue. Over his shoulder was one of the gifts she had made, and she recognized it instantly as being the symbol of the Arapaho tribe. Thad interpreted for her as she listened.

"Chief Nakos of the Arapaho tribe says, 'You bring kindness and friendship to our tribe, and we thank you.'"

Next to him, a woman appeared, carrying the handkerchief Betsy had made for her, saying much the same thing. Betsy was touched as Thad interpreted for her. The tears that had gathered wouldn't be kept at bay for long.

The Cheyenne chief was next, then the Crow and the Blackfoot. Others followed.

Then Joseph stepped forward with a bow.

"I'll call you the Bride of White Panther as the Sioux, and say "You have a heart of generosity and kindness. You've noticed the needs of those around you. And you've worked hard to meet them. You made my Evie much happier. *I* failed to notice her needs in the little place she calls home, but *you* didn't. You noticed it the first time you were there. And you fixed it by making it a pretty place for her. You gave her a sanctuary she loves, and you made us both happy. We will be wed soon, and it will be our home. Thank you."

Thad brought out a handkerchief from his pocket. It was one Betsy had made, and she laughed when she saw it. It was then Suzy and Andrew moved into her field of vision, smiling.

But it was Suzy who began.

"Oh, Betsy. You've taught me what it's like to care for others," she said with a sob in her voice, "and you've shown that care in so many ways. I promise to learn from you. Thank you, my friend."

"You brought peace among us again. Thank you." Andrew added, next to Suzy.

Permelia and Cordelia, followed by Father O'Leary, expressed their sentiments as well. Even Evie had worked her way outside and taken her place beside Joseph, saying her thanks.

The very last person to come forward was one she never expected. Betsy's expression changed as she saw Henry Lake in front of her. His black eyes flashing and his thick shock of black hair falling almost over his eyes, he gave her a quick nod.

"Damn good poker player."

* * *

When Joseph stepped forward with a large package in his hand, he handed it to Thad.

"For the Bride of White Panther."

Betsy eyed the package, swallowing with a hard gulp.

"Open it," Suzy suggested, from the crowd.

With a glance at Thad, Betsy began pulling the ribbon from the package. Once it was removed, the wrapping fell away. Thad held the box as she lifted the top.

And gasped with pleasure.

The long red velvet cape was folded carefully, the same one she'd admired in Joseph's front window at the Trading Post. Thad took his jacket from her shoulders, and then replaced it with the scarlet cape from the package. Quickly he wrapped her in it, bringing the fur-lined hood over her head to frame her face; then leaned down to kiss her forehead.

"This is not from me, sweetheart," he said softly. "It's from *them*."

Joseph grinned. "For you. From us."

"*All* of us," added Chief Swift Eagle.

Betsy couldn't keep back the tears any longer. Now, she was crying in earnest. When the crowd began to speak among themselves with concern, Thad explained they need not fear; she was crying because she was so happy, and so touched.

"I..." She looked up toward the throng of people, "I don't know what to say."

Thad hugged her closely to him as he leaned down into her ear. "Just say thank you, sweetheart."

Betsy glanced around the crowd at the smiling faces, some weathered, some with Indian dress, some with uniforms. But all full of gentleness, Yet each of them had come together for a single purpose; to express their thanks and their love.

Wrapping her arms around her husband, she drew

comfort from him before turning back to the crowd of smiling faces.

"Thank you," she whispered, with tears of joy running down her face. "*Thank you all.*"

Joseph waited until the crowd had thinned out and came forward, and Betsy turned to Evie. "I think my mother's wedding dress might fit you," she whispered softly. Please let me know what else I can do." But Joseph leaned forward.

"You can talk tomorrow," he said softly. "I'm taking Evie home now. It's cold out here and you two need some time alone. And Thad?"

"Yes?"

"Go easy on her."

Thad's response was a nod.

Joseph left with Evie as Thad took her into the house. "Come with me, sweetheart," he said softly.

As he closed the door behind them, she balked.

"I... can't seem to get my feet to move."

"Shall I carry you?"

She looked up into his face. He didn't look angry, but she knew she was in trouble. "What are you going to do?" Her voice was barely above a whisper.

Thad smiled as he picked her up. "You'll see."

She half expected him to put her over his knee, but instead, he set her in his lap gently and cradled her in his arms.

"What are you *expecting* me to do?" he asked.

"I don't know."

"Elizabeth," he said softly, "I'd be an ogre if I insisted on spanking you after all I've heard this afternoon. Half of it, I didn't even know about. My heart burst with pride when I heard the words of those who expressed their thanks. And you've added peace between so many of the tribes and the white man, not just for what you did yesterday, but for the gifts you'd already sent ahead. You've accomplished a peace treaty all by yourself with your love and your care for others, in ways I *never could* have. He laughed, suddenly. "Even Henry Lake was impressed."

Betsy blinked, her face full of wariness, and Thad continued.

"No. You're safe this time, sweetheart. Although, you'd better understand, future poker games are out of the question. And when I send you into the tunnel, I'll expect to find you there when I return. Not standing in the pathway of two hundred arrows. Understand?"

"I understand, sir."

He bent to kiss her temple, then her mouth, as he

rose with her in his arms. "And now, he said softly, "I'm taking you to bed. As Joseph suggested, I need time alone..."

"Yes?" she added, waiting, and above her, he smiled.

"With the *Bride of White Panther*."

The End